William Kelly

The harp without the crown

William Kelly

The harp without the crown

ISBN/EAN: 9783744736954

Printed in Europe, USA, Canada, Australia, Japan

Cover: Foto ©Andreas Hilbeck / pixelio.de

More available books at **www.hansebooks.com**

THE

HARP WITHOUT THE CROWN,

OR

Mountcashel's Fair Daughter.

AN

IRISH HISTORICAL DRAMA

IN FOUR ACTS,

By WILLIAM KELLY.

NEW YORK:
FRANCIS AND LOUTREL, STEAM JOB PRINTERS AND STATIONERS,
No. 45 MAIDEN LANE.

1867.

DRAMATIS PERSONÆ.

LORD MOUNTCASHEL, ...General of the Irish Army.
ST. RUTH,..........In Command of the French and Irish Troops.
MARSHALL LUXEMBURGH, Commander-in-Chief of French Troops.
CAVALIER PHILABERT EMANUEL DE TESSEE, Second in Command.
DUKE OF TYRCONNELL,......Viceroy of Ireland Under K. James.
SARSFIELD, EARL OF LUCAN,.....Major Gen'l of the Irish Army.
SIR DERMOD O'BRIEN,.....Colonel of the Fourth Irish Dragoons.
COLONEL GRACE,.........Commander of the Fortress of Athlone.
COLONEL FITZGERALD,......Commander of the Irish Grenadiers.
O'DONNELL,.. ...
DILLON,..
O'NEIL,... ....
COL. DORRINGTON, Commander of the Royal Irish Foot Guards.
FATHER O'CARROLL,.... ..Chaplain to the Mountcashel Family.
MICHAEL O'RYAN,................ Sergeant in Sarsfield's Own.
ONEY SHEEHAN,..............................An Irish Piper.
O'CARROLL OF NENAGH,..............Leader of the Rapparees.
TIM O'CONNOR,......................Of the Kilkenny Rangers.
RORY,..
COLONEL HERBERT, ...Of King William's Army.
MAJOR GENERAL DOUGLAS,.......Commanding English Troops.
GENERAL REVIGNY, ... A Huguenot.
GENERAL LEEVISON,.....Commander of the Dutch Blue Guards.
SIR TOBY BUTLER,..........Commander of Ormond's Yoemanry.
STAFF OFFICERS,....................................
FIRST and SECOND ENGLISH SOLDIERS........... ....
LADY EVILEEN MACCARTHY,.......Daughter of Lord Mountcashel.
NORAH O'LEARY,.................Foster-sister of Lady Evileen.
WIDOW SHEEHAN,.............................Mother of Oney.
OFFICERS, SOLDIERS, RAPPAREES, YOEMEN, PEASANTS, &c., &c.

ACT 1.

SCENE I.—Interior of Ballymore Castle, residence of the Mountcashel Family.

SARSFIELD, EARL OF LUCAN,......Major Gen'l of the Irish Army.
SIR DERMOD O'BRIEN,.....Colonel of the Fourth Irish Dragoons.
COLONEL GRACE,.........Commander of the Fortress of Athlone.
COLONEL FITZGERALD,......Commander of the Irish Grenadiers.
MICHAEL O'RYAN,................Sergeant in Sarsfield's Own.
ONEY SHEEHAN,............................An Irish Piper.
COLONEL HERBERT,................Of King William's Army.
LADY EVILEEN MACCARTHY,.......Daughter of Lord Mountcashel.
NORAH O'LEARY,................Foster-sister of Lady Evileen.

Lady Evileen weeping.

Norah.—There, now, sweet Lady, do have courage, you will kill yourself intirely—so you will, alannah. They dare not touch a hair of your father's head. Come, asthore machree, let your poor Norah once more see you look happy.

Lady Evileen.—Thanks, dear Norah; I will try to compose myself. But, Norah, when I realize the fact that my poor father is wounded, and in the hands of his enemies, far away from those he loves so well—no kind voice to cheer, no gentle hand to tend his wounds—my courage fails me. If I could but watch by his couch, I would then indeed be happy.

N.—Sweet lady, but that cannot be; so come, now, cheer up alannah. You know how unhappy you would make your father if he was aware that you were fretting and crying yourself sick. Are you not a MacCarthy? Is he not suffering in a good cause—the cause of our poor old country, her liberty and her faith? So do, acushla, do cheer up and look happy once more.

Lady E.—Thank you, kind Norah, I will endeavor to do as you wish.

N.—Ah, that does my heart good to hear you speak so cheerful—and you know there's Sir Dermod, what would he say if he saw you frettin so—for shure he loves the ground you walk on, and dotes on your name; God bless him, but he's the prince of a gentleman.

Lady E.—Stop, stop now, I will get jealous. God grant this war may soon be ended, and peace restored to our poor country. Oh! father dear, your child prays for comfort and consolation to your lonely heart.

N.—Hush, hush, did you not hear? Listen! yes, it is the messenger from Dublin. God grant he brings us good news.   [*Exit Norah.*]

[*Enter Norah.*]

N.—Oh, a letter for you. Open it quick my lady.

[*Lady Evileen takes the letter and looks at the directions.*]

Oh, Norah dear, it is from Sir Dermod.

[*Kisses it, opens and reads.*]

"Dublin, Tuesday night, June 5th, 1690.

"My beloved Evileen,—All is lost. After a long, and bloody struggle at the Boyne, we have been defeated, and are in full retreat. I hope soon to have the happiness of seeing you. Heard from your beloved father; he is rapidly improving, and is treated with kindness by our enemies. In haste, yours devotedly,

"Dermod O'Brien."

N.—Now, my Lady, you must look like yourself again.

Lady E.—Yes, yes, kind Norah, but this is bad news for our poor country. May God strengthen her children, and bless them with courage and strength to battle with our enemies.

N.—Yes, may Heaven bless them, and pity those that have lost sons, brothers and lovers. Oh! Michael! Michael! Do you think he has escaped, my Lady?

[*Norah weeps.*]

Lady E.—Come, come, Norah, do not be alarmed; your lover has escaped, I feel confident.

[*Enter Servant. Announces Sir Dermod O'Brien.*]

[*Enter Sir Dermod. Lady Evileen rushes to meet him. They embrace.*]

Lady E.—Dermod, dear Dermod.

Sir D.—Evileen, my dear, this, indeed, is happiness; but, darling, how changed you look. I fear the news of your beloved father's capture has preyed severely on you.

Lady E.—Dear Dermod, I will promise not to think so often of it; but come, Dermod, tell me the news from Dublin?

Sir D.—Oh, dear Evileen, it is bad news. The King, for whom we have sacrificed all, is fled to France, and left us to struggle against the mercenary hordes of the Prince of Orange.

Lady E.—It will, indeed, be an unequal struggle.

Sir D.—Yes, but better make the sacrifice than surrender our liberty and our ancient faith.

Lady E.—Nobly spoken, dear Dermod. God will bless our arms.

Sir D.—Our brave Sarsfield has assumed command of our shattered, but not beaten army—he is infusing new life and spirits into the troops, and declares he will contest every foot of ground against the invaders of our country.

Lady E.—And my poor father cannot assist you.

Sir D.—That may not be so; he will soon be exchanged, and then we shall again have the benefit of his wise council and brave sword.

Lady E.—But tell me, Dermod, your brave dragoons, I hope, have not suffered severely. My poor foster-sister is most unhappy about her lover.

Sir D.—His name, Norah.

N.—Michael O'Ryan, your honor.

Sir D.—Michael, ah, yes; why that must be Sergeant Michael O'Ryan of my regiment. He is safe, and as sound as a bell, I am happy to tell you, Norah, and will soon be in the neighborhood—he is as brave a soldier as ever put foot in stirrup. Now, dear Evileen, time presses, I must make my adieus. Farewell, till to-morrow.   [*Exit Sir Dermod.*]

SCENE II.—Grounds and Castle of Ballymore.

[*Enter Sergeant Michael O'Ryan, singing:*]

Oh, I am a bowld dragoon,
With my long sword, saddle, bridle,
Whack, rowdy, dow.

Sergeant O'Ryan.—Ah, thin, musha, the Lord be thanked that I live to lay my two liven eyes on the ould Castle of Ballymore again. God presarve its ould walls, and the people that live under its roof; and shure they are the rale ould stock—none of your half-and-halfs. Not a drop of blood in their vanes that's not as purely Irish as my own, and that's saying a good deal. Ah! God be good to my poor father's soul, for he used to tell me, "Mickey, my boy, niver disgrace the dacent name you bear; for," says he, "in the churchyards of Ballinaclouch and Dollardstown there is some tombs of your ancesters as ould as Mathusalah, and a good deal oulder." And there's the sweet Lady Evileen, she's an angel, so good to the poor on the estate, and the colleen that's to be Mrs. O'Ryan.

[*Enter Oney Sheehan.*]

Serg't. O'R.—Ah, Oney, my poor boy, how's every inch of yourself, and the pipes. I hope you'r doin a thrivin business.

Oney.—Och, thin, Master Michael, honey, but the good ould times are changed intirely since the theevin red coats came amongst us, with their Dutch pretenders and there Hessians. Shure it's one wake and one chrisinin in a month now, and as for weddins, shure the like is not thought of these days.

Oh, sweet bad luck to the invaders of our country, and God bless King James and the great Louis of France, of brave ould France, the ould friend of our nation.

Serg't O'R.—You are right, Oney, my boy, he is the friend of our poor ould country. I see you wear the ould cockade, Oney.

Oney.—Wear it, och thin may I niver die a sinner but I'll wear it 'till the hour of me death.

Serg't O'R.—How's the poor ould mother, Oney?

Oney.—Ah, thin bless you, avick, for askin', but she's mighty poorly. Ould age is coming on her mighty quick, and these troublesome times worries the poor ould soul.

Serg't O'R.—And the ladies at the castle, Oney, when have you been up there?

Oney.—Ah, God bless the cratures, they've always a welcome for the poor piper, and the sweet colleen with her own hands, filled out the tay for my breakfast, the crature asked me fifty-five questions about the news that's a goin'. I tould her the King had run away.

Serg't O'R.—What did she say to that?

Oney.—" Oney," says, she " betune you and I he's no great loss." Then she asked me when did I think the boys woul be coming to Ballymore, and told me to come to the castle and let her know when Sarsfield's lads come to the neighborhood.

Serg't O'R.—God bless her. Oney will you do me a little taste of a favor?

Oney.—Ah, thin Michael my honey, shure I'd walk on my knees for you.

Serg't O'R.—Well, now take this little taste of a paper to the colleen. [*Trumpets sound.*]

Serg't O'R.—Ah ha! that's the general's call.

Oney.—Is it Sarsfield's?

Sarg't O'R.—Yes, Oney, my boy; its our brave Sarsfield—God bless him.

Oney.—Amen. [*Exit Oney.*

SCENE III.—*Sarsfield's camp—with the Irish National Flag and the flag of France.—Sentry pacing to and fro.*

[*Enter Sarsfield from his tent. Orderly hands dispatches. Reads.*]

Sarsfield.—Alas! 'tis too true: James, our unfortunate King, has indeed fled. Coward, double coward; to thus fly from a devoted and confiding people, who have staked all in his service—their lives, fortunes, and national existence. Oh! base ingratitude;—yes, Tyrconnell may cry treason; but Ireland, our beloved land, has first claims on our devoted loyalty. Yes, yes, all is not yet lost. We fight now for Independence and civil and religious liberty, and to that sacred cause, my life, my fortune and my honor, I consecrate.

[*Trumpets sound. Enter Colonel Grace, Colonel Fitzgerald, and Sir Dermod O'Brien. Sarsfield advances to meet them.*]

S.—Welcome, gentlemen, welcome. [*Shakes them heartily by the hand.*] Delighted to see my old comrades in arms. What news?

Col. Grace.—On the receipt of your dispatch we have hastened to receive your instructions.

S.—Thanks, gentlemen, for your promptness. Time is indeed precious. Our enemies are vigilant and active. The Prince of Orange is already on the march to Limerick. Major-General Douglas is concentrating a large army, and has advanced as far as Mullingar. Now, gentlemen, I will take care of Limerick, be it yours to protect the lines of the Shannon. Our grand centre, the fortress of Athlone, Colonel Grace, into your hands I commit its defence. Colonel O'Brien, with two Cavalry Brigades, will guard with sleepless diligence the passes of Ballymore, Banagher, and Lainsborough. Athlone must once again bid defiance to the persecutors of our race. To you, Sir Dermod, I commit the defence of my old friend's home, the Castle of Ballymore, and its precious inmate, the Lady

Evileen, and see that no rude mercenary of William's defile with his presence the stately halls of Mount-cashel, Clancarthy or Muskerry. Sir Dermod, you will at once throw out scouts, and report to us the movements of our crafty enemy. I have sent a dispatch to the brave O'Carroll of Nenagh, and his bold rapparees to harass and obstruct their advance. Now, gentlemen, at to morrow's dawn we will resume our march to Limerick. May heaven guide our councils, and strengthen our arms, to strike home the enemies of our well beloved land. Farewell.

[*Exit Sarsfield, Grace & Fitzgerald*]
[*Enter Sergt. O'R.*]

Col. O'B.—Sergeant O'Ryan; you know the country well from here to Mullingar?

Serg't O'R.—Know it, your honor! Ah, can a duck swim, your honor. Ah, shure there's not a blade of grass from this to that that Mickey Ryan doesn't know; for many a time, when I was a gassoon, I traveled that same road, and a mighty crooked one it is, your honor.

Col. O'B.—Very good, Sergeant. Take twenty men with you and scout; but be careful and vigilant, as you have a crafty foe to deal with. I will follow with my brigade. Be careful; I again enjoin you.

Serg't O'R.—O, God bless your honor, the red coats won't catch Mickey Ryan sleeping. [*Exit.*]

SCENE IV.—The English camp—A group of officers —General Douglas and staff.

[*Enter Sir Toby Butler—Gen'l Douglas advances to meet him.*]

Gen. D.—Welcome, my worthy friend; the Prince of Orange commands me to express to you his profound gratitude, for your valuable services in his cause.

Sir Toby.—Ah, thank you, General; but the house of Ormond only does its duty. It has always upheld the glory of old England, right or wrong. Aha, the rebel rascals; we must teach them civilization, General. Aha, civilize them, General; that's the way to fetch the rascals. My brother, Lord Ormond, has commissioned me to offer to the Prince of Orange the services of the Kilkenny Rangers—a cavalry corps raised from his tenantry; they know the country well, and will, I flatter myself, under my command, General, do the cause of the prince good service.

[*Gen. Douglas takes Sir Toby's hand.*]

Gen. D.—Your services are most gratefully accepted.

[*Drums beat; trumpets sound. Enter staff officer.*]

Officer.—A sergeant of the enemy's has been taken prisoner, whom the commander of the fort has no doubt is a spy, as he was taken within our lines.

Gen. D.—Bring him into our presence immediately.

[*Enter Colonel Herbert, with Sergeant O'Ryan handcuffed.*]

Col. H.—This is the prisoner.

Gen D.—Well, my fine fellow, what have you to say for yourself? How came you within our lines?

Serg't O'R.—Bedad, yer honor, I got a little drop in my head and it got the better of me; devil a bit but it did, yer honor,—so that when I thought I was on the straight road to Athlone shure I was turnin' my back to it all the time, yer honor. Bad luck to such a mistake as that has Mickey Ryan made since he was christened, and shure that's over twenty years ago, yer honor.

Gen. D.—That's all very fine, my man; but the fact of your being taken within our lines places you in a bad position. A court martial will assemble immediately, when you can make your defence, but the fact of your being a spy leaves little doubt that you will have to suffer the penalty of death. What regiment do you belong to?

Serg't O'R.—To the Fourth Irish Dragoons. Sarsfiell's Own, your Honor—the finest regiment in King James' sarvice, God bless him and bother his enemies.

Sir Toby.—Ha! you rascal: hold your Jacobite tongue; we'll teach you how to speak to gentlemen. Aha, that we will.

Officer.—Keep a civil tongue in your head, you Irish Jacobite.

Serg't O'R.—Musha, then, you dirty spalpeen, if you just take off those things, and stand out there before me, I'll dust your dirty carkass for you in quick sticks. You pack of dirty rebels, I'll teach yees dacent manners, and not to insult a poor boy when his hands are tied.   [*The officers return to the front of the stage in consultation.*]

Gen. D.—Prisoner, it is my painful duty to inform you that you have been found guilty of being a spy. The laws of war are short, and swift, and at five to-morrow morning you will be shot, and God have mercy on your soul. Colonel Herbert; you will take the prisoner in charge.   [*Exit.*

Serg't O'R.—Oh, Norah, darling, must I die and not see your face, or speak one word to you, darling; it is but a short time your poor boy has to live, alannah. Oh, Father Patt, if I could but get your blessing I would die happy. Oh, Norah, darling. Hush, Mickey my boy; have courage; you must not let your enemies think you are afraid to die a soldier's death, or disgrace the decent name you bear.

Col. H.—Prisoner, there is one way to save your life. You can give us some valuable information. Your life is in your own hands.

Serg't O'R.—No, your honor; my life belongs to my country. Turn informer, on the poor ould land of my birth. Oh! God forbid. I would die a thousand deaths first. No, Norah darling; your poor boy will die like an Irish soldier—true to his country and his colleen. Lead on, your honor, I am ready to die.

SCENE V.—A wild mountain scene—The moon seen through large mass of clouds—The English camp in the distance—Firing party, in charge of Col. Herbert—The muskets stacked—Serg't O'R. and guard dosing asleep—Oney's pipes are heard in the distance.

Serg't O'R. starts; the Lord be good to me; if that's not Oney Sheehan's pipes I'm not a living boy.

[*Sentry, awakening, asks what music is that.*]

Serg't O'R.—That music. Don't be frightened avick, for I think it's the fairies that are on the march, for they never travel without music.

Sentry.—Fairies! man. What are they?

Serg't O'R.—Oh, then avick, where were you born, or what kind of cultivation did your mother give you? Don't know what the fairies are! Well, I will enlighten you. They are the good people.

Sentry.—What good people? what good people? Good people, indeed, in this infernal country. Why, you are all a parcel of dunderheads, who refuse to receive our good Saxon civilization.

Serg't O'R.—Now be aisy, avick. I can't stand that. Is it civilization ye mane? It's jonking ye are. Isn't ould Ireland the land of Saints and Shamrocks. Civilization, indeed. Ah, be easy my boy. Hundreds of years ago, didn't Saint Patrick (God bless him) send his Saints across the sea to teach yous Christianity and dacency. Didn't King Dathy conquer the world, and only he died at the foot of the Alps he would have conquered China too. Ah, be aisy; Julius Cæsar conquered yees and made yees his slaves, but he never set foot in ould Ireland, as good reason why, because we wouldn't let him. And there's Saint Bridget; didn't her Habit cover the Currough of Kildare. I spose you never heard of that mirical. Well, I will tell you. Saint Bridget was traveling in the Sweet County of Kildare, and King O'Toole, of course, hearing she was coming his way

like a dacent Christian went to pay his obadience to
the Saint; and the King, having a son born to him
with a reel foot, the cunning old fox thought he'd ax
the Saint to cure him. Well, be dad; Saint Bridget
said she would if he'd give her as much ground, to
build a church, as her mantel would cover. It's a
bargain, says the King. Well, but the Lord preserve
us, the Saint's mantle spread over the whole Currough
of Kildare, and on it was built great churches and
monasteries. The Saint, God bless her, had the best
of the bargain.

[*Noise is heard. The sentry springs to his feet and
seizes his musket. Enter Oney Sheehan.*]

Sentry.—Who goes there?

Oney.- ·It's only the poor piper.

Sentry.—Stand and give the countersign or I'll blow
your brains out.

Serg't O'R.—Ah then now, sentry honey, don't
harm the poor piper; shure he's an omadhaun, and
don't know what the countersign manes. Shure the
poor boy has no sinse in his head—goes round the
counthry playing his pipes for the bit he ates. Let
him pass; sorra harm he'd do yees, barren you might
get a little information out of him.

Sentry.—He don't look much like a chap that could
do much harm; so come, sit down and play us a tune.
[*Oney plays.*]

Oney.—Michael, alannah, the boys are marchin'
on us.

[*Here the guards fall asleep. Oney steals along and
pours the water from his chanter on the priming of
the muskets. In a few moments the heads of the Irish
soldiers are seen cautiously advancing. They rush on
the stage. The guards awake, rush to their muskets,
but they will not go off. Michael is unbound, and the
English officers and men are taken prisoners by the
Irish troops.*]

SCENE VI.—Interior of Ballymore Castle, with windows looking out on the road. Trumpets sound, drums beat.

[*Enter Sir Dermod O'Brien, Lady Evileen, Norah, Sergeant O'Ryan, and attendants.*]

Sir D.—Evileen, dear, our troops are preparing to move. Knowing how pleased you would be to see them depart must be my excuse for disturbing you so early this morning.

Lady E.—A thousand thanks, dear Dermod: ten thousand thanks.   [*Trumpets sound.*]

Serg't O'R.—Ah! there, your honor. There's the last call. See, see, the boys are already moving. [*The band is heard playing Garryowen.*]

Serg't O'R.—Ah, gineral, jewel, there goes Tyrconnell's Own, all yellow bellies, every man sowl o' them: they are the boys that can push the bayonet. There's Dorrington's Royal Foot Guards—County Louth boys—every man six foot in his stocking feet. Here comes Sir Art. Maguire's regiment—County Antrim boys. There goes Sir Phelix O'Neil, with his Rangers; and, sir, there goes Marshal Lautzen, and our brave friends the French: how lovely they march: you'd think every man was a dancing-master, they keep such purty time. Ah, here's Sarsfield and his staff: a long life to him; he looks the jewel of a soldier. Hear how the boys cheer him. There goes the Kerry Artillery, every man of them as active as the goats of their native mountains.

[*The ladies join in the general enthusiasm, during which the curtain falls.*]

END OF ACT I.

ACT II.

SCENE 1.—Interior of Ballymore Castle.

SARSFIELD, EARL OF LUCAN,.. ....Major Gen'l of the Irish Army.
SIR DERMOD O'BRIEN,.....Colonel of the Fourth Irish Dragoons.
O'DONNELL,.......................... ...
MICHAEL O'RYAN,............... ... Sergeant in Sarsfield's Own.
ONEY SHEEHAN,..........................An Irish Piper,
TIM O'CONNOR,....................Of the Kilkenny Rangers.
RORY,..................................
COLONEL HERBERT,.................. ...Of King William's Army.
FIRST and SECOND ENGLISH SOLDIERS........... ....
STAFF OFFICER,.............................
LADY EVILEEN MACCARTHY,.......Daughter of Lord Mountcashel.
NORAH O'LEARY,................. ...Foster-sister of Lady Evileen.

[Enter Lady Evileen and Norah O'Leary.]

Lady E.—Oh, this dreadful suspense. Oh, Dermod, dear Dermod, may Heaven shield you in this fearful conflict. The loud boom of cannon all this morning tells with a dreadful certainty that the conflict rages with unabated and stubborn fury. Oh, father dear, your child feels desolate in this crisis of our country's struggle; for if Athlone falls, then Ballymore must fall, and your child will be houseless, and the home of the MacCarthys will become the prey of our ruthless enemies

Norah.—Oh, lady dear, it breaks poor Norah's heart to hear you speak so sorrowfully. Do cheer up; the boys will fight bravely, and may good Saint Bridget pray and look on our poor country in these dreadful times.

2

Lady E.—Hush! Did you not hear the sound of horses' feet? Ring the bell, Norah.

[*Enter Servant.*]

Lady E.—Any news yet, Rory?

Rory.—No, my lady.

Lady E.—Then, send Father O'Carroll to me.

Rory.—He's not in the castle, my lady.

Lady E.—Not in the castle? When did he leave?

Rory.—At daybreak this morning, for Athlone, to attend the wounded of our army.

Lady E.—Noble Priest! may God strengthen him, and send our brave soldiers victory.

[*Loud cheers are heard. Enter Sir Dermod O'Brien and Serg't O'R., with Col. Herbert as prisoner. Dermod and Evileen embrace. Serg't O'Ryan and Norah embrace.*]

Sir D.—Dear Evileen, God has given us the victory. Douglas is in full retreat, and Athlone is saved.

Lady E.—Thank heaven! But our brave troops must have suffered dreadfully.

Sir D.—Yes; our enemy fought with dogged and determined bravery.

[*Bows to Col. Herbert, and introduces him to Lady Evileen.*]

Lady E.—Col. Grace, I hope, is not hurt.

Sir D.—No, dear Evileen, though it is a miracle how he escaped, being exposed to a terrible fire from the enemies' batteries; but he seemed to have a charmed life. Wherever the battle raged fiercest he was to be seen encouraging and animating our troops. At four in the morning, the enemy made a most determined effort to ford the Shannon, at Lainsborough. My brigade dismounted, well protected by breastworks, poured a murderous fire on the advancing foe, which staggered the advancing column; but, being rallied by their officers, again formed, and boldly charged our position; now ensued a desperate struggle, but the fire from our line being murderous, the enemy staggered and fell into partial confusion. Perceiving our turn had come, I gave orders for the boys to form and charge the enemy. The rout was complete. Numbers were drowned in the vain attempt to re-cross the Shannon. Douglas, seeing the impossibility of carrying our position, gave orders for the retreat. Col. Grace, delighted with our success, sent orders for me to join him, with all dispatch, by the Ballinasloe Road, as he was confident that Douglas would now concentrate all his strength and attempt to force our position at Irishtown; and events proved that he was right, for, at eleven, Douglas pushed a solid column of seven thousand of his best infantry, supported by his well appointed and splendid batteries. Our kinsman, the brave Fitzgerald, with his brigade of Irish Grenadiers, met the shock of the advancing host, and, for two hours, foiled their bravest efforts to effect a landing. Douglas, seeing that the column made but little progress, gave orders for his reserves to move; and, placing himself at the head of the William's Dutch Blue Guards, the finest regiment in the enemy's service, dashed across the river. The struggle now became desperate and bloody. But in the meantime, Fitzgerald being reinforced by Dorrington's Brigade of Royal Irish foot guards and McMahon's Brigade of regulars, gave our boys hope and courage. Oh, Evileen, the fate of Athlone hung on a thread, and you may well imagine the thoughts and feelings of its heroic old commander as he caught sight of our dragoons, as we dashed into the town. Placing himself at their head, and with one wild cheer for Sarsfield and King James, we dashed at the foe, who had by that time forded the river. The shock was terrible and irresistible. The enemy were beaten and Athlone was saved. But, dear Evileen, our brave friend Michael is wounded; we must see to him.

[*Turn round and see Michael and Norah talking.*]

Serg't O'R.—Ah, long life to your honor. Shure I'm as happy as a grand Turk. Shure the colleen, your honor, is attending me, with her own little taper fingers, and there seems to be healing plaster on them, your honor, for the pain goes away when she touches me.

Lady E.—Dermod, dear, you must send for the doctor to see to Michael's wound.

Serg't O'R.—Heaven bless your ladyship for your kindness; it's just a little taste of a scratch; sorra ha'p'orth more your ladyship; it's nothing to the other wound I received.

Sir D.—Michael, you did not tell me of that before. I insist on sending for the doctor.

Serg't O'R.—Yer honor is wounded, deeply wounded, too; in troth you are, your honor.

Sir D.—Me; me. Where?

Serg't O'R.—Ahem! [*Takes Norah's hand; puts it on his heart.*] Your honor, there is no use in sending for the doctor; the cure is here, your honor.

[*Sir Dermod takes Lady Evileen's hand; they laugh heartily.*]

Serg't O'R.—Ah, your honor, it is a most vulnerable part—always exposed to the round shot of a purty pair of eyes.

Sir D.—Lady Evileen, Col. Herbert will remain a prisoner, on parole of honor.

Lady E.—Col. Herbert, you will, I trust, make your stay with us as free from restraint as possible. Our library is at your service. The grounds around the castle will, I hope, interest you.

Sir D.—We wish to make your stay with us as pleasant as possible, until you are exchanged. The Lady Evileen cheerfully extends to you the hospitalities of the house of Mountcashel; the Earl, her father, being a prisoner of war in the hands of your friends.

Col. H.—Allow me to express to the fair lady my sincere thanks for her kind invitation, which I cheerfully accept. Thanks, also, to you, Sir Dermod, for your gentlemanly and soldierly conduct, and if my services can be of any use, now or hereafter, you can, at all times command them. I will write to England, to my brother, Lord Herbert, who is high in the confidence of the prince of Orange, our future king, interceding for a speedy exchange of Lord Mountcashel.

Sir D.—You are very kind Col.

[*Enter a dragoon with a dispatch—hands it to Sir Dermod—he reads:*]

LIMERICK, Midnight, August 2d, 1690.

Sir Dermod—Douglas has re-inforced William before Limerick. Loose not a moment in joining us with your Brigade. Cross the Shannon at Killaloe.

Ever faithfully yours,

PATRICK SARSFIELD.

P. S.—Express to the Lady Evileen my respects and sympathy.

Sir D.—Ah, such is a soldier's life. Evileen, my love in ten minutes I must be in the saddle on my way to our friends.

Lady E.—Dear Dermod, you will not leave us so soon.

Sir D.—Ah, would it were possible for me to tarry a little longer, but when duty calls we must obey. Our enemies are active and vigilant, and then Sarsfield requests me to lose no time. Oh, my love, our country owes him indeed a debt of gratitude, he is the life and soul of our army; and from a confused mass has organized and built up an army full of national spirit and bravery, fully competent to drive back from old Limerick's walls, the mercenaries of England, and my sweet Lady Evileen I am sure has the interest of our country too much at heart to ask a soldier to neglect his duty. [*They embrace.*]

Lady E. [*weeping.*]—Go Dermod darling, though my heart should break, and may heaven shield and guard you from your enemies, and soon restore to our afflicted country. happiness and peace.

[*Exit Sir Dermod and Lady Evileen.*]

Serg't O'R.—Amen, say I, and may the divil run jumpin' with the red coats—the curse of Cromwell light on them and their civilization, as they call it, we want none of it, nor their judges with their big wigs, and their sheriffs with their long staffs, as they call them; if they'd only just have the dacency to let our little

2 *

island alone, how happy we would be, Norah darling, ah, shure you'd be Mrs. O'Ryan before this time, and we'd both be sleeping under the same roof together, as happy as two young doves in a barley stack. But never mind alannah, we'll be a thorn in their side any how. It's not crying you are, Norah darling?

Norah.—You are going to leave me again Michael, and may be I never may lay an eye on you again.

Serg't O'R.—Arah, by Saint Patrick you will lay two eyes on me, and two bright ones they are, may God bless them and the love that's in them for your soldier boy. [*Gives her a kiss.*] Many a better man died for ould Ireland, [*Gives her another kiss*] Norah darling.

Norah.—Stop now, Michael, what would father O'Carroll say if he saw you behave in this way?

Serg't. O'R.—Ah, then, his reverence, God bless him, would'nt say a cross word to me. Shure, it was only the other day at the fight at Athlone, that he came up to me just as the red coats were running away; "Mickey, my boy," says he, "I am proud of you, the Garyowen boys fought like Trojans. Kneel down till I give you my blessing." So, bedad Norah darling, don't be making yourself in the least uneasy, but fearing that you would, I just take them back to ease your conscience, [*Kisses her,*] good by, my poor colleen. [*Shakes hands. Norah weeps.*] Don't cry alannah.

Norah.—You wont forget your poor Norah.

Serg't. O'R.—Forget you, Norah, darling? Never, alannah, while grass grows or water runs.

Col. H.—[*Who had remained a spectator of this interview.*] Well, fellow, how long will I have to listen to your nonsense.

Serg't. O'R.—Well, now, who the divil thought a fine gentleman like yourself would listen to a poor boy taken leave of his colleen, there are plenty of other things to take your honor's attention; the fine pictures there on the walls.

Col. H.—Fellow, you don't seem to know who I am?

Serg't. O'R.—I am no fellow, I don't wear a wig; I am Sergeant of Dragoons, in the Fourth Irish

Sarsfield's Own, long life to him, and bad luck to his enemies; just amuse yourself looking at the pictures, while I speak a few words to the colleen.

Col. II—They are, indeed, splendidly executed. Ah! what a noble looking fellow; I say, my man, whose portrait is that?

Serg't. O'R.—That? Ah! that's the Lord himself, God bless him.

Col. II.—What Lord?

Sergt. O'R.—What Lord? Why Lord Mountcashel, who else would it be. And that's his kindsman, Lord Muskerry, and there's his brother Lord Clancarthy, and here is the sweet Lady herself, an angel, and nothing short of it, your honor.

Col. II.—Yes, a lovely face indeed, but proud and haughty, like all the Irish upstarts.

Sergt. O'R.—Come, your honor must not speak disrespectfully of the fair daughter of Mountcashel, while Mickey Ryan is by to defend her and the honor of her house.

Col. II.—Fellow, you are impertenant.

Sergt. O'R.—Hould now, I told you before I was no fellow; say but one undasent word against that sweet Lady, and I'll dust your red coat for you without a beesom.

Col. II.—I cannot tolerate this impudence, you don't seem to know who I am.

Sergt. O'R.—Ah, that's easy found out by the color of your coat; shure you are one of the tormenters of ould Ireland, who wants to be Lords of the lands, and ride rough shod over our liberties and religion.

Col. II.—Impudent babbler, I'll teach you to respect your superiors! [*Draws his sword. Serg't O'R. draws his.*]

Norah to Serg't O'R.—Oh, Michael, darling, as you love your Norah, don't mind him avick; with your poor wounded arm, what could you do alannah?

Serg't O'R.—Stand back, Norah acushla, it's only a scratch. [*They fight. Serg't O'R. disarms Col. II. Sir Dermod and Lady Evileen rush in and save the life of Col. II. Just at this moment the clear notes of a trumpet call is heard.*]

SCENE II.—Oney Sheehan's cottage. Oney is heard playing on his pipes. Enter Sergt. O'R., singing,

Oh my name is Paul Dougherty, from the north country,
Where there's a still upon every stream,
Landlady be quicker, and bring us more liquor,
And bring us a juice that is stronger than cream.

Ah, poor Paul! he was the life of our boys: he fell by my side at the Boyne; didn't get as much time to live as you'd say Lord have mercy on me.

Oney —Och, Michael, honey, long life to you.

Serg't O'R.- Same to you, my boy; and how is your poor mother, the creathur?

Oney.—She's poorly avick; but these times we must be thankful if we are alive at all, at all.

Serg't O'R.—True for you, Oney; they are bad times, and I fear there's worse in store for us.

Oney.—Don't say so, avick. I hope the good cause will prosper in spite of our enemies.

Serg't O'R.—I hope so, Oney my boy. I am going to Limerick.

Oney.—To Limerick! I'll go there, too; I can fight.

Serg't O'R.—What! and lave your poor mother just on the verge of the grave. No, my boy, you can be of more use at home. Listen: stay around the castle. Keep your ears and eyes open; know every thing, but seem to know nothing: you understand. Act the omadhaun, but to the cause be faithful and vigilant. There is now at the castle one of our persecutors: watch his movements in our absence. If any move is made, don't spare brogue-leather or wind to let us know of it. Here, take these two sparrow-killers, you may need them some time [*Puts out his hand and shakes hands*]. Good bye, Oney, my boy; be true to the ould cause.   [*Exit Serg't O'R.*

Oney [takes out his green and white cockade, fixes it in his coat, and looks on it with admiration].—True to the ould cause. Yes, with my life; I pray for it night and day. [*A voice is heard crying " Oney. Oney."*] Yes, mother, honey, I'm coming.   [*Exit Oney.*

SCENE III.— Camp of the Irish army near Limerick —Arms stacked and soldiers lying around—Trumpets sound the call for dinner—The men jump up.

Tim O'Carroll.—Now, boys, there's the dinner call. [*Enter Serg't O'Ryan.*]

Serg't O'R.—How are yees, boys ; and how are yees making it out these times.

Tim O'C.—Well, Sergeant, jewel, plenty of marching and digging, and just as much to eat as keeps body and sowl together; but shure its all for the good of ould Ireland, and we don't grumble, Sergeant, jewel. Any good news agoing ?

Serg't O'R.—Yes, boys, the cause looks bright, and our friends are hopeful, and the Dutchman's getting out of temper at our stubborn defence. Come, boys, fix up a table—I've got a snug little present for yees—a bottle of real ould potheen. [*Cheers from the boys.*] Sit down, boys, and we'll have a song. [*Cheers from the boys again.*]

Tim O'C.—Take your seats, every mother's sowl of yees. Sergeant O'Ryan for the Widow Malone. [*Cheers from the boys again.*]

Serg't O'R.—Well, boys, I'll do my best to plaze yees. [*Cheers again—Michael sings.*]

> Oh, then, did you e'er hear of the Widow Malone,
> Ochone,
> Who lived in the town of Athlone,
> Alone ;
> Och, she melted all hearts of the swains in those parts,
> So lovely was Widow Malone,
> Ochone,
> So lovely was Widow Malone.
>
> Of lovers she had a full score,
> Or more,
> And fortunes they all had galore,
> In store ;
> From the major down to the clerk of the crown,
> All were courting the Widow Malone,
> Ochone,
> All were courting the Widow Malone.

But so modest was Widow Malone,
            'Twas known,
No one could ever see her alone,
            Ochone;
Let them ogle and sigh, they could ne'er catch her eye,
So bashful was Widow Malone,
            Ochone,
   So bashful was Widow Malone.

Till one Sergeant O'Brien from Clare,
            How quare,
Shure it's little for shyness they care,
            Down there,
Put his arm round her waist, gave ten kisses at least,
Oh, says he, you're my Molly Malone,
            My own,
   Och, says he, you're my Molly Malone.

And the widow they all thought so shy,
            In my eye,
Ne'er thought of a simper or sigh,
            For why;
But, Michael, says she, since you have now made so free,
You may marry your Widow Malone,
            Ochone,
   You may marry your Widow Malone.

There's a moral contained in my song,
            Not wrong,
And, one comfort, it's not very long,
            But strong;
If for widows you die, learn to kiss, not to sigh,
For they're all like your sweet Molly Malone,
            Ochone,
   Oh, they're all like sweet Molly Malone.

[*The boys give him a cheer. Just then a noise is heard. A voice cries, I must see him. Oney Sheehan rushes on the stage, his pipes tied on his back, covered with mud.*]

Serg't O'R.—Good Saint Bridget defend me. Oney, my boy, where did you come from?

Oney.—A long way, Sergeant jewel.

Serg't O'R.—What, in the name of all that's holy, brought you all this way from home?

Oney.—The cause that I'd die for brought me here, Sergeant, jewel. Is Sir Dermod O'Brien here? I have a small taste of a letter for him from Lady Evileen.

She towld me, the Angel, so she did, that life and death was in my hands. Here's the letter, Sergeant.

Serg't O'R.—Ha! this must, indeed, be something important. Sit down, Oney, avick, and rest yourself, for you seem sadly in need of it.

[*Enter Sir Dermod. Sergeant O'R. hands him the letter. Reads.*]

" BALLYMORE CASTLE, August 10th, 1690.

DEAR DERMOD :—The brave O'Carroll, of Nenagh, has this moment visited the castle in disguise. He tells me William's siege train and supplies have just quitted Mullingar. They go by the mountain road, so as to avoid your cavalry. Some parties of English troops were in the neighborhood yesterday. Sir Toby Butler's yeomanry are getting troublesome. I send this by Oney, in whose fidelity and cunning to baffle the enemy I have the greatest confidence. Praying that God will shield you and bless our sacred cause, I remain yours, ever. EVILEEN MACCARTHY.

Sir D.—Oh, bless her; bless her. [*Kisses the letter.*] Sarsfield must see this dispatch at once. Sergeant, get your troops in order.

[*Enter Sarsfield, map in hand.*]

Sir Dermod.—My Lord, I have just received this dispatch.

Sarsfield.—[*Reads*] Bravely done, Noble daughter of Mountcashel; this is indeed most timely and valuable news; for by my spurs this train must never reach the Dutchman. Sound the call, Sir Dermod, and to horse: we take the Fourth Irish, that will suffice. [*Opens the map*]. Yes, we cross the Shannon at Killaloe. Tarry not nor tighten rein till we reach the mountains; then may heaven send us the victory. [*Exit.*]

*SCENE IV.—Ballyneedy—A wild mountain road—
The English train at a halt ; arms stacked.*

First English Soldier.—I say, John, what a confounded wild country this is ! I'd give a crown piece to be safe out of it. What if those confounded Rapparees, as they call 'em, were to pounce on us in such a wild place.

Second English Soldier.—Ah, the scoundrels, they know better than to attack us regulars; we'd blow them to atoms, the thieving Jacobites. When our brave Bill brings his guns to bear on Limerick he'll make short work of the rascals.

[*A loud volley of musketry is heard, and the cheers of Sarsfield's troops, as they dash on the astonished foe. The English give way and surrender to Sarsfield—General Mackey taken prisoner.*]

Sarsfield.—Sir Dermod give orders to boviac for the night. At morning's dawn we return to Limerick. See to our own and the enemy's wounded. Our troops are weary after their long ride, and require a little rest. Post your sentrys, with the injunction to be vigilant. Yes, our victory is complete, and Limerick saved from the hand of the invader.

Sir D.—We have taken four six-pounders, six twelve-pounders, and four twenty-pound siege guns, and one hundred and fifty-three wagons of ammunition and stores.

Sarsfield.—The spoils were worth the risk, Sir Dermod. Our cause looks bright, and our flag—the harp without the crown—will yet be thrown to the breeze, and upheld against all comers. Oh may that day soon arrive, for in good truth I am weary of all English factions and parties, be they of the house of Orange or the House of Stuart ;—they all use us alike. After giving our fortunes and our lives with a devotion and profusion unequaled in the annals of history, what has been our reward ? Witness the ungrateful and cruel conduct of Charles the Second ;

death, neglect and confiscation were all we received for our loyalty then ! What do we receive now ? Ah, but little indeed ! Tyrconnell may cry treason, but my heart and my conscience tell me that to love Ireland before all, and above all, is no treason.

[*Exit Sarsfield and Sir Dermod. Sergeant O'R., in charge of the guard, walks up and down the stage; sings,*

> The young May moon is beaming love,
> While half the world is dreaming love ;
> How sweet to rove through Moira's Grove
> While the drowsy world is dreaming love.

Ah, then, Mickey my boy, you feel purty drowsy now avick, and shure its no miracle that you would, after seventeen hours in the saddle ; divil such ridin' since I took to sogerin ; up hill and down hill, helter skelter. Ah, the gineral, God bless him, he never spares horse flesh when he's after the red coats. Bedad I'll take a wink or two. [*Spreads his coat on the ground and lies down.*] Begorra it's mighty strange—I feel drowsy, but I can't get a wink of sleep.

[*Oney's pipes are heard playing.*]

Serg't O'R.—By all that's wonderful if that's not Oney Sheehan's pipes I'm not a living boy. Oh, by Saint Bridget, there it is again. Whist !

[*Enter Oney.*]

Oney.—Is it asleep you are this blessed night. The red coats have crossed the Shannon at O'Brien's Bridge, and they will be in Cullen in less time than it takes me to tell you. Fly, or it will be too late.

Serg't O'R.—God bless you, Oney, my boy.

[*The trumpets sound the call. Enter Sarsfield.*]

Sars.—Quick, my men, unpack the ammunition waggons ; load the guns to the mussels ; scatter the powder barrels ; round the wagons. See that nothing escapes. Then make your train. Mount, men, quickly ; our crafty foe will find the spoils gone. All ready ?

Sir D.—Yes, sir.

Sars.—Apply the match. Now for Limerick. [*A loud report is heard, and scene changes.*]

3

SCENE IV.—Battlements of Limerick—Hills of Clare, and the Shannon in the distance—Cannonading and volleys of musketry. Enter Sarsfield, O'Brien, O'Donnell, and staff.]

[*Enter Staff Officer.*]
Staff-Officer.—The enemy in strong force have assaulted our first lines of intrenchments. The fight rages fiercely. They are pushing large masses of infantry on our right.

O'D.—General, permit me to move out with my regiment and reinforce Dorrington—the Red hand will show his banner to the Dutchman.

Sars.—Bravely said, my friend. Colonel Dillon's regiment shall accompany you.

O'D. [*taking Sarsfield's hand.*]—Farewell, General.
[*Exit Dillon and O'Donnell.*

[*Enter Staff Officer.*]
Staff Of.—The enemy have carried our first line of works.

Sars.—Ride for your life, sir. Tell O'Donnell to fall back.
[*Exit officer.*

[*Enter officer.*]
Of.—The enemy have attacked our second line furiously with a strong column of Huguenots and Blandenburghs, six thousand strong. They defy all our efforts to check them.

Sars.—William grows angry. This is his best card, but it will not avail him [*Enter Dorrington.*] General, summon the citizens to our assistance.
[*Exit Dorrington.*

[*Enter citizens, men and women, drawing cannon. Enter Dorrington.*]
D.—The Blandenburghs have advanced to the Black Battery.

Sars.—Then tell O'Brien to fall back, and fire the mine. Now our turn comes. [*A loud report is heard*

—*Sarsfield draws his sword.*] Soldiers, the foe is at our gates. They must be driven back at all hazard. Show our flag to the Dutchman. Forward! for Garryowen and victory.

[*Cheers and shouts. The fight goes on. The crowd of combatants drive back the enemy, and are driven in return. The English troops are driven out of Limerick. Cheers from the Irish troops. Enter Sarsfield, Dorrington, officers and soldiers—citizens, women, &c., who are received with enthusiasm. Enter O'Brien and Serg't O'Ryan.*

O'B.—General our victory is complete. The enemy are in full retreat. Limerick is saved.

[*Cheers, during which the curtain falls*]

END OF ACT II.

ACT III.

SCENE I.—City of Limerick—Thomond Bridge—French Fleet at anchor—Troops drawn up on the quays—Irish Flag and Royal Ensign—Drums beat—General Dorrington in command—The Duke of Tyrconnell, Sarsfield, Dillon and Officers in waiting—Saint Ruth passes through the gangway—Soldiers present arms—Band plays, "See the Conquering Hero Comes."

ST. RUTH,..........In Command of the French and Irish Troops.
DUKE OF TYRCONNELL,......Viceroy of Ireland Under K. James.
SARSFIELD, EARL OF LUCAN, ...Major Gen'l of the Irish Army.
DILLON, ...
O'NEIL,.. ....
COL. DORRINGTON, Commander of the Royal Irish Foot Guards.
SIR DERMOD O'BRIEN,.....Colonel of the Fourth Irish Dragoons.
FATHER O'CARROLL.. ... ..Chaplain to the Mountcashel Family.
MICHAEL O'RYAN,............. .. Sergeant in Sarsfield's Own.
ONEY SHEEHAN,.... ....An Irish Piper,
RORY,.... ....
CAVALIER PHILABERT EMANUEL DE TESSEE, Second in Command.
COLONEL HERBERT, ...Of King William's Army.
SIR TOBY BUTLER,..........Commander of Ormond's Yoemanry.
STAFF OFFICERS,........................... .. ..
DRAGOONS,..
LADY EVILEEN MACCARTHY,......Daughter of Lord Mountcashel.
NORAH O'LEARY,..... ... ...Foster-sister of Lady Evileen.
WIDOW SHEEHAN,.... ....Mother of Oney.

Tyr.—Welcome, Saint Ruth. [*Introduces Saint Ruth to all the officers.*]

St. Ruth.—Gentlemen, my royal master, at the urgent solicitation of your lawful King, has appointed me Commander-in-Chief of the Armies of Ireland and

France. The King has commanded me to express to you his profound gratitude for your faithful and devoted loyalty to his house. Gentlemen, I solicit your co-operation and assistance in the good work we have so deeply at heart. [*Shakes hands with all the officers.*]

Tyr.—To the castle, general; you must need repose. To-morrow we hold a council of war.

[*Soldiers march off stage. Exit all.*]

SCENE II.—*Council Chamber in Saint John's Castle. Sentry on guard.*

[*Enter Tyrconnell, arm-in-arm with Saint Ruth— Sarsfield, O'Brien, Dillon, O'Neil, Dorrington, and other officers. Tyrconnell occupies the chair.*]

Tyr.—Gentlemen, I feel a pleasure in thus meeting so many of my old comrades in arms. The cause we all have so much at heart, I am happy to tell you, looks bright and hopeful. The arrival of our friends is most opportune, and in my judgment our best course will be to immediately assume the offensive. It will keep alive the fine spirit now existing in our army. But we are here to ascertain the opinions of the gentlemen present. What says our brave friend Saint Ruth?

St. Ruth.—My Lord, I am decidedly opposed to assuming the offensive at present. My troops require rest. There is no need for any forward movement for at least two weeks to come.

O'B.—I agree with his Excellency, we ought to assume the offensive without a moment's delay.

O'N.—I coincide with his Excellency. [*A knock at the door. Tyrconnell gives orders to the sentry to open it. Enter Sergeant O'Ryan, excited—Speaks with Sir Dermod and retires. Sir Dermod speaks with Sarsfield.*]

3*

Sars.—I favor an immediate advance. Ginkle has already pushed forward to within a short distance of Athlone. The fortress and castle of Ballymore are in the enemy's hands. The home of my old friend, Lord Mountcashel, is garrisoned by the foe. Your Excellency, in my opinion, we ought long since to have been on the march. Our friends in the Counties of Meath, Westmeath, Kings, Queens and Tipperary already feel the scourge of the invaders. Sir Toby Butler, with his partizan yeomanry, kill, plunder and burn indiscriminately. Let me beseech of our brave Commander-in-Chief to adopt our advice and council.

St. R.—Gentlemen, I think you all overrate the strength of the enemy. When I am ready to move they will soon feel my power. When Saint Ruth marches he marches to victory.

Tyr.—Then, General, we wait your pleasure. The council is ended.

[*Saint Ruth and Tyrconnell retire as they entered, arm-in-arm. Sarsfield, Sir Dermod, and O'Neil, remain.*]

Sars. [*taking Sir Dermod's hand*]—I sympathize with you; but the Lady Evileen will be treated as her position deserves: bad as are our enemies, they dare not offer her any insult.

Sir D.—That may be so; but, General, her noble spirit will feel deeply the humiliation; for it is indeed, humiliating to see the red cross float from the stately battlements of Mountcashel.

Sars.—Yes, yes; this cruel infliction would have been spared us had Saint Ruth taken our advice. Oh, my country, thou art a toy in the hands of these men, tossed and played for like a thing that has no life, no heart, no claim to an existence or a nationality. William, cruel and crafty, would have us vassals to the House of Orange—James, imbecile and feeble, vassals to the House of Stuart—Louis, well meaning and generous, would use us to advance his interests and the glory of France. Oh, O'Brien, how I long and pray for the hour to arrive when our people will unfurl their flag—the harp without the crown. Oh, may that day soon arrive.   [*Exit.*]

SCENE   III.— Widow Sheehan's   Cottage—Mountains in the distance.

[*Enter Oney, playing his pipes—takes out his cockade, looks at it admiringly, and fixes it on his coat.   Noise is heard—Oney, alarmed, takes it off and hides it away.*]

Oney.—The Lord presarve us these dreadful times. 'Tis sartin death if the cockade is seen now. Arrah, but bad luck has come intirely on the good cause since the French came last. Hush! [*A drum is heard.*]   It's the yeomen.   [*Exit.*]

[*Enter Sir Toby Butler with a company of yeomen.*]

Sir T.—Aha; I think we'll have him this time. Aha, my fine fellow, caught in your own trap, at last, pipes and all, I'll wager my honor. [*Knocks at the cottage door.   No answer.*]   Eh; come, come, open the door at once, or we'll soon break it in for you.

Widow Sheehan [*speaking from the window*].—Ah, thin, what would so fine a gentleman, like your honor, want with the poor widow this blessed day?

Sir Toby.—Come, old woman, none of your palaver or equivocation. We want your son, so open the door at once.

Widow S.—My son, your honor, has gone to Athlone to buy a little tay and tobacco for the onld woman, yer honor.

Sir T.—He's in the house, so open the door at once; if not we'll soon take means.—Here, sergeant, get some dry straw; we'll smoke them out; we'll soon fetch these Jacobites—aha! aha!   The piper

won't go round the country playing his treasonable
tunes and ridiculing the British .constitution and its
noble king.   Aha! we'll have him this time.

Widow S.—Oh, your honor wouldn't set fire to our
little cabin over our heads?

Sir T.—Apply the match, sergeant. [*Just then
Oney and his mother are seen making their escape.*]
Aha! aha! there they go. Ready—aim—fire. [*At
the first volley Oney's mother falls. Oney takes her in
his arms and moves up the mountain.*] Load. Ready
—aim—fire! [*When the smoke clears away Oney
has escaped, bearing with him the lifeless body of his
mother.*] By heaven he has escaped us again !

                                              [*Exit.*

—   - - -

SCENE IV.—*Interior of Ballymore Castle.*

[*Enter Lady Evileen and Norah O'Leary.*]
Norah—Come now, my lady, shure the boys will
soon be coming from Limerick, with the great French
general at their head, to relieve us from the red
coats. Mavourneen, do now let your Norah see you
look happy again.

Lady E.—'Tis impossible. How can you expect it,
Norah. I will leave the castle to-morrow, and retire
to Roscommon Castle. We will be near our friends
then, Norah. Yes, I have made up my mind, Norah.
Please ring for Rory. [*Norah rings. Enter Rory.*]
Tell Col. Herbert I wish to speak with him. [*Exit
Rory. Enter Col. Herbert.*] Col. Herbert, I have
taken the liberty of requesting an interview. My object in so doing is to inform you that I with my
attendants leave the castle to-morrow.

Col. H., [*aside*—Never, except as my wife.*] You
astonish me.   I hope none of the attendants has
given your ladyship any cause of complaint, for I

had given strict orders for every attention and respect
to be paid to your ladyship.

Lady E.—I am resolved to leave to-morrow.

Col. H.—It will be impossible. You cannot leave.
The most imperative orders from head-quarters state
that you must not be permitted to quit the castle.
You seem astonished, but, lady. I hold his majesty's
commission and must obey his orders.

Lady E. [*turning to Norah*]—Now, indeed, is our
cup of bitterness full. [*Embraces Norah and weeps.*]

[*Enter Sir Toby.*]

Sir T.—Aha, aha, Colonel—glad to see you. [*Puts
out his hand to shake hands. The Colonel reluctantly
takes it.*] What do you think, Colonel, but that
rascal of a piper has escaped me once more—aha, aha.

Lady E. and Norah.—Thank God he has.

Col. H. [*walks to the other end of stage*]—Confound
the old fool, I wish him far enough this moment.

Sir. T.—But his old hog of a mother I think must
be shot.

Lady E. and Norah.—Shot! the poor Widow
Sheehan. By whose orders?

Sir T.—By mine. She tried my patience sorely,
and brought it on herself—aha, aha. That she did.

Lady E.—May heaven defend our poor people from
such petty tyrants.

Sir. T.—Come, my fine young lady, recollect who
you speak to.

Norah.—Come, my fine ould tyrant, recollect that
when you speak to the daughter of Mountcashel you
must speak with dacency; but shure what can be ex-
pected from the murderer of a poor defenceless old
woman, you ould rat trap. You have not the courage
of a soldier, but rove round the country murdering
poor defenceless people. It's well for your ould bones
that I wear petticoats.

[*Sir T. gets in a rage.*]

Col. H.- Pardon me, Sir Toby, we soldiers are here
not to make war on the ladies, but against men with
arms in their hands, who are disputing the authority

of his majesty. I have some little business to arrange at present. Any other time I will be happy to see Sir Toby Butler.

[*Exit Sir Toby, looking quite insulted.*]

Lady E.—By whose orders am I detained a prisoner in my father's castle ? Oh, father, your child is heart-broken and desolate!

Col. H.—I beg you will allow your maid to withdraw, as I wish to speak to you alone.

Lady E.—I cannot grant your request. My foster-sister shares with me my sorrows and my pleasures. No secrets are hidden from my faithful Norah.

[*They embrace.*]

Col. H.—Be it so, fair lady. Then to be brief—I love you. Do not start, fair Evileen. From the moment I had the happiness of seeing you, this heart has loved you with a fondness I cannot describe. In vain I endeavored to reason and argue with myself against its rashness—its foolishness, if I can so call it ;—but love triumphed over all reasoning, and now, when you are, I might say, left without a protector in these troublesome and uncertain times, I offer you my hand and fortune. My brother, Lord Herbert, is unmarried, old and feeble, and according to the rules of nature cannot live long. At his death you shall share with me the coronet of a peer of England. This war will not continue long. Then the two people will become united, prosperous, and happy. May I hope for a favorable answer from my fair Evileen.

Lady E.—Colonel Herbert, I will be brief. My affections are already given to another, I, when a child, being betrothed to Sir Dermod O'Brien. The strong ties of honor and duty, the old friendship between the Houses Mountcashel and Inchiquin bind and seal the contract then made, which nothing but death can undo. Of my father's misfortune and this evil war I shall say nothing. Colonel, you are, I am sure, too honorable to press your suit further after this explanation.

[*Enter dragoon with despatches. Hands them to Col. Herbert. Col. Herbert opens the despatches and reads:*

"The enemy were feeling our position to-day with a brigade of cavalry, under Sir Dermod O'Brien. There was some slight skirmishing, which brought on a severe action, in which we lost a goodly number of men. It was reported Sir Dermod was killed, which report was afterwards confirmed by some prisoners. Keep your troops well in hand, as the enemy is moving.

"Yours in haste,

"GINKLE, *Maj.-General.*"

Col. H. [*aside*]—This is indeed most opportune. She shall know it. [*Reads the despatch. Lady E. falls into the arms of Norah and is borne to her chamber.*] Now, Evileen, I will press my suit. Yes, she must be mine. [*Exit.*

SCENE V.—*Ball-room in Roscommon Castle—Band playing—Saint Ruth and all his officers, Tyrconnell, and ladies—The pleasures of the night at full blast. Enter Sarsfield—Trumpets sound; drums beat; the dancing ceases.*

Sars.—Cease these sounds of revelry and to your posts, gentlemen. The enemy is before Athlone. If Colonel Grace is not reinforced, and that quickly, it must fall.

St. Ruth.—Go on with the dance. Tell them Saint Ruth is near.

Sars.—I implore you, General, to send reinforcements without delay.

St. Ruth.—There is no danger. Let the festivities be resumed.

Sars.—Oh! my country, thy destiny is in the hands of a vain but brave man, who knows not the subtle foes he has to deal with.   *[Exit Sarsfield.*

[Enter staff officer.]

Staff Of.—General, the enemy has forded the Shannon in three columns. Fitzgerald, with his grenadiers, makes a gallant resistance, but must be soon overpowered.

St. Ruth.—Stop the festivities! To your posts, gentlemen *[takes out his watch.]* At five let the advance guard move forward.

[Enter Sarsfield.]

Sars.—Athlone is lost. The red cross of Saint George floats from its historic and time-honored walls. Its brave commander sleeps the sleep of death. Oh, Saint Ruth, thy laxity has cost our poor country dear.

St. Ruth.—Such language to your superior ill becomes you.

Sars.—Draw and defend yourself.

[They cross swords. Tyrconnell on one side and Dorrington on the other interpose their swords between the combatants.]

Tyrconnell.—Gentlemen, I pray of you to desist.

[Enter staff officer.]

Staff Of.—The enemy has crossed the river in full force. Their pickets are posted one mile from our camp.

St. Ruth.—Sarsfield, I was wrong *[proffers his hand]*; forgive me. Let us be friends *[looks at the map]*. Yes, yes, that will be my position, and all the efforts of the enemy will be unavailing to move me from it. Gentlemen, we'll move at once for Aughrim, near Kilcomnadan Hill—there our position will be impregnable.   *[Exit.*

*SCENE VI.—Battle of Aughrim, July 12, 1691—St.
Ruth's tent—The green flag and French flag displayed—Sentry on guard.   Enter Sarsfield, Dorrington, the Cavalier Philibert Emanuel De Tessee,
(second in command to Saint Ruth), and Saint
Ruth.*

St. Ruth.—Gentlemen, I have called you together
to receive my final instructions for the coming conflict; for I feel morally certain that the enemy will
attack us at the coming morrow. Our position I con-
sider impregnable. You will act on the defensive
until you receive further orders from me. Gentlemen,
I enjoin you to be vigilant and keep your troops well
in the position I have marked out for you. I pray
God will send us the victory. I have yet much to
arrange.   With the assurances of my regard I will
dismiss Good night, gentlemen.   [*Exit Sarsfield
and other officers. The sentry walks on his post.
After the lapse of a few moments the trumpets sound.
Enter St. Ruth from his tent.*]
    St. Ruth.—Ha! there goes Sarsfield's summons to
the strife. The enemy must be on the move.
    [*Enter staff officer.*]
    Staff Of.—The enemy has made a furious effort to
force the passage of Urrachree with two squadrons
of Danish dragoons, but were quickly driven back,
and were as quickly reinforced by Sir Albert Cun-
ningham's regiment of dragoons, who attempted to
make a flank movement. Sarsfield gave orders to
O'Brien to fall back as if retreating. The enemy,
deceived, crossed the ford and charged. O'Brien
quickly faced about, reinforced by Maxwell's regiment, and charged the enemy in return; but the
struggle was brief. The English troops gave ground,
and re-crossed the ford. The enemy now quickly sent
Eppenger's royal regiment of Hollanders to the rescue,
but nothing could check our noble boys. The
enemy were, meantime, becoming rapidly disor-
4

ganized, when, as a last resource, the Earl of Portland's
Royal House Guards were ordered to the rescue, to
make a last effort to save and retrieve the day. Oh,
General, it was a sight never to be forgotten to see
that splendid regiment, six hundred strong, advance
to the charge. My heart failed me for our brave
boys, and I felt spell-bound; but then rung out, on
the clear morning breeze, the well-known bugle
charge of Sarsfield's Own. On they came, with the
Earl at their head. The shock was terrific. The
struggle, short and bloody, ended in the complete route
of the enemy. Under your orders, General Sarsfield
did not pursue the retreating foe.

St. Ruth.—Ah, now I divine Ginkle's intention to
flank by Urrachree. He has been foiled. Ride
out, sir, and give our best thanks to General Sarsfield,
with orders to let nothing tempt him to leave his
position.   [*Exit staff officer.*

*Distant canon—rollies of musketry—St. Ruth paces
the stage, glass in hand; looks through it.*

[*Enter staff officer.*]
Staff Of.—Major-General Mackay's division has assaulted our entrenched position in front of Kilconn-
dar Hill. The fight rages. The enemy has massed
large bodies of troops on our left and left centre.

St. Ruth.—So much the better, sir. The cannonade
grows furious. My horse! I will ride over the field.
                          [*Exit. The firing ceases.*

[*Enter Saint Ruth.*]
St. Ruth.—Yes, they are beaten! I will drive them
to the gates of Dublin.

[*Enter staff officer.*]
Staff Of.—Mackay is retreating after desperate
efforts to carry the pass of Aughrim. The enemy's
cavalry are massing in front of the castle, but Sir
Walter Burke keeps them in check.

St. Ruth.—Good, sir! good! Viva la France, viva
la Ireland! My horse! our time has come to assume
the offensive.   [*Exit.*

[*Enter De Tessee and staff.*]

De Tessee.—Our Brave countryman, St. Ruth, is dead! Oh! misfortune! misfortune!

[*Enter staff officer.*]

Staff Of.—Our Troops are dispirited : they look for Saint Ruth.

[*Enter staff officer.*]

Staff Of.—The enemy has massed all his available troops, reserve and all, in front of the position held by the French troops.

De Tessee.—I will ride out, sir.   [*Is struck dead.*

[*Enter Sarsfield.*]

Sars.—O'Neil! O'Neil! Saint Ruth has fallen! All I fear is lost [*turns to staff officer*]. Go, sir, find General De Tessee. [*Exit officer.*] Yes, yes, he may rally his countrymen, and we may yet triumph.

[*Enter staff officer.*]

Staff Of.—The brave De Tessee has fallen. His efforts to rally his countrymen were fruitless.

Sars.—Ride for your life, sir!—Tell Sir Walter Burke to keep the enemy's cavalry engaged at all hazards. Tell Hamilton, Mansfield and Dorrington to fall back slowly.

[*Enter Sir Dermod O'Brien.*]

Sir D.—General, the French troops are disorganized and numbers have been taken prisoners.

Sars.—Ha! But we can fight and beat them yet.

Sir D.—'Tis not possible, now, the French in their efforts to escape have become a confused mass, and all attempts to rally them is fruitless?

Sars.—I feared some sad result like this. Why did Saint Ruth keep us in ignorance of his plan of battle! Go, O'Neil, and Dorrington, and by your presence animate our brave troops. Keep the enemy in check while we complete our arrangements to fall back. O'Brien, concentrate all your available cavalry—keep the enemy engaged. Oh! my country! this is a sad day for thee.

[*Enter staff officer.*]

Staff Of.—The enemy manœuvres to cut off our retreat to Limerick.

Sars.—Ha! The crafty foe this time at least will be foiled. Ride back, sir: tell General Mansfield to deploy his light battery across the Ballinasloe road and give the enemy a plentiful supply of grape shot. Colonel O'Reilly's regiment will support him. Loughrea will be our rallying point. [*Enter Staff officer.*] Well, sir! [*Staff officer hands him a dispatch.*] The infantry have fallen back in good order, but suffered severely.

Sir D.—We want your orders.

Sars.—Keep the enemy's attention engaged, sir, till I join you. [*Exit Sir D. Sarsfield turns to orderly.*] Who has charge of Saint Ruth's body?

Orderly.—It has not been found, sir, as yet.

Sars.—It must be found—brave son of France. Yes, we leave some of Ireland's noblest and best unburied and unhonored, but France must not say the Irish troops paid no respect to her distinguished son. Sound Sarsfield's call [*draws his sword.*] Forward, my boys! Victory or death! [*Exit.*

Fighting is heard. The Irish troops are driven on the stage; the English fall back in return. The Irish troops again come on the stage. Six men with their muskets crossed bear the lifeless body of Saint Ruth. They fight, keep the English at bay, while they carry away the body in triumph.

SCENE VII.—Field of Aughrim the morning after the battle. Castle of Aughrim in the distance.

[*Enter Lady Erileen, dressed in black, Norah, and Father O'Carroll, chaplain to Lord Mountcashel. Norah carries a basket with lint and restoratives for the wounded.*]

Father O'C.—Here, my children, the struggle must have been most desperate and bloody. Let me entreat of you to turn away and resume our flight, the enemy may soon be coming this way. Such sights are not fitted for your gentle natures.

Lady E.—But, good father, we may save the life of some of our soldiers: yes, perhaps many lives. Hush! did you not hear a moan? Listen, Norah. [*Norah listens.*] There it is again. Let us proceed, good father.

[*They walk to the end of the stage. The moan is repeated.*]

Norah.—Good Saint Bridget protect us, but I have heard that voice before. Hush! [*It is repeated this time more distinctly.*] It is merciful. [*Norah runs from the stage. She cries for help. Exit. Re-enter Father O'Carroll, helping on the stage Serg't O'Ryan, wounded, Norah weeping. They lay him resting on the stage and give him some restoratives.*] Michael avick machree, don't you know me. Do speak one word to your own colleen: one word Michael. Ochone, ochone, why was I born for this sorrow.

Father O'C.—Norah, you must have patience; the poor fellow is stunned, and weak from the loss of blood. Patience, my child! [*They bind up his arm. Norah weeps. Michael opens his eyes and draws a deep sigh.*]

Serg't O'R.—Where am I? Where is Sarsfield? where's Saint Ruth? Where's the flag!—the flag! Am I in a dream? Why am I alive?

Norah.—Michael, avick machree, won't you spake? you'll break my heart!

Serg't O'R.—Oh, that I died a thousand deaths!—but I did, I did [*puts his hand in his bosom*]; it is here [*draws out the flag and opens it*] thank God, oh good Saint Patrick be blessed and thanked [*kneels on the stage and kisses the flag*]. The flag of Sarsfield's Own—the Harp without the Crown! Norah, my darling, forgive your poor boy [*they embrace*]. Shure allannah I was bewildered out of my wits [*kisses her —turns to Lady Erileen—takes off his hat*]. The sweet lady will excuse my bad manners in not paying

4*

my respects to the fair daughter of Mountcashel and
his riverence.

Lady E.—His reverence, Michael, will give you
his blessing.

Father O'C.—God bless you, my boy. May you
always love the old flag with the same devotion. You
had a narrow escape, my boy.

Serg't O'R.—Ah then it's true for your riverence ;
but that last charge beat Bannagher, and shure Bannagher
beats the divil. Such fightin' Mickey Ryan
niver saw afore. Led on by the French orderly to
where Saint Ruth fell, we dashed up the hill. The
foe poured on us a perfect deluge of shot ; but that
didn't stop us, divil a bit of it your riverence, and the
enemy seemed to think so, too, for they sent two
regiments of Danish dragoons, every man of 'em six
feet in his stockings, big omadhauns with iron waist-
coats and iron helmets on their heads. Then came the
tug of war. The poor divils caught it, any how. For
the one blow they could give, our boys gave them two,
being light and handy, handling their swords as if
they were bits of shillelahs. Poor Lieut. O'Donohue
fell dead by my side, and I hadn't time to say Lord
have mercy on him before the other ensign, young
O'Reilly, of Budda, shared the same fate. As he fell
I snatched the flag, and at that moment I received this
cut on my arm from a big Hessian who made a
desperate cut at me. I parried it, but the blow severed
the flag from the staff. He then drew his pistol and
fired, but my poor horse, rearing at the instant, received the discharge in his head, when after a few
violent plunges we both fell together, stunning me
so badly that I ceased to remember any more.

[*The distant sound of a drum is heard.*]

Father O'C.—Ha ! the enemy are astir.

[*Enter Oney Sheehan.*]

Oney.—Fly ! fly ! The red coats seek you on every
hill and valley. Sir Toby, with his murderers, are on
the hunt for yees. Colonel Herbert swears vengeance.
Fly ! or it will be too late.

Father O'C.—Let us away, my children ; the fo· is certainly near.

[*The drum is now heard approaching nearer.*]

Oney.—Ah, there's the yeomenry, the murderin' thieves ; but, Sir Toby Butler, I'll have revenge yet. Yes, mother jewel, I'll have satisfaction on your murderer. I'll track him like a bloodhound by night and by day, over hills, through the valleys, across rivers and seas, through every parish and barony, from Onneybeg to Coolagh, from Clanwilliam to Small County, from Coshlea to Coshma, from Pobble Brien to Upper Connells, from Lower Connells to Kerry, from Kerry to Kilmallock. Oney will know no rest till this murderin' ould wretch feels my vengeance.

Father O'C.—Oney, my poor boy, you must forgive your enemies. Come, take some nourishment.

Oney.—Your riverence, I have no appetite. My heart is sick and sorrowful, and I feel no hunger but the hunger for revenge. Ah! forgive my poor mother's murderer—never! What pity has he for our poor people, who are shot down like dogs.

[*At this moment a voice is heard crying "Surrender, you Jacobite dogs! Surrender!" Enter Sir Toby Butler and yeomanry. Oney and Sergeant O'Ryan fly up the hill.*]

Sir T.—Aha, aha. There goes the rascals. Ready—aim—fire!

[*Just then Michael is heard cheering, waving his flag. Another volley fired by the yoemen, but Michael and Oney escape.*]

Sir T.—By heaven they have escaped me this time, too : but who have we here? Aha! a nice place for the ladies this! And you, sir : how come you here? Give an account of yourself, sir.

Father O'C.—I am a clergyman—chaplain to the Lord Mountcashel.

Sir T.—Aha, aha! A fine Jacobite that ; but he's done for. Aha, aha! Well, you'll have to come along with me. I'll find a place where you will be safe. Aha, aha!

Father O'C.—We are going to Limerick, sir. By what authority do you detain us?

Sir T.—By the King's authority, sir. Here, sergeant, put handcuffs on those Jacobites. We'll teach them to be loyal to the British Crown.

Father O'C.—You don't mean to put those disgraceful things on the lady's hands?

Sir T.—Yes, sir Sergeant, do your duty.

Father O'C. [*taking his stand before the ladies*]— Back, sir! back! I am a man of God and peace. Seventy winters have passed over my head; but to accomplish this wanton insult to the fair daughter of Mountcashel, you must pass over my lifeless body [*takes Lady Evileen to his side*]. Back, sir! back! [*Just then drums are heard. Enter Col. Herbert, officers and soldiers*] I appeal to you, Colonel Herbert, to prevent this wanton insult.

Col. H.—What is the meaning of all this?

Sir T.—These Jacobites are my prisoners. They must be handcuffed and taken to Ballybracken Jail.

Col. H.—Sir Toby Butler, you make a great mistake I am in command of this district, and these people are *my* prisoners. Shame on you! Those ladies are now under my protection [*advances and takes Lady Evileen's hand*]. Lady, be under no apprehension. No insult shall be given to the Lady Evileen. Why did you leave your home? Return, I beseech you, to the castle. To Limerick you cannot go. Our troops have possession of the whole country from here to the very gates of that doomed city. You would probably meet with nothing but insult from our rude soldiery. Father O'Carroll will, I am sure, agree with me.

Father O'C.—If Colonel Herbert pledges his word of honor that no insult will be offered, I certainly will advise the Lady Evileen to return to the castle.

Lady E.—Good father, I will do as you advise.

Col. H.—Then let us depart. There is every indication of a coming storm.

[*They prepare to move.*]

Sir T.—Colonel Herbert, these people are my prisoners, and I claim their custody, sir. Yes, sir, I insist on you giving them up to me. Yes, sir, I insist on it. I have the means to compel you, sir. Ahem! Attention, my men! Shoulder arms!

Col. H.—Recollect, sir, you now have his majesty's troops to contend with, and not the poor unarmed peasantry. Put up your muskets, sir. The first man that fires will hang from the nearest tree. Come, ladies. *[Exit Col. Herbert and ladies.*

Sir T.—Fire! *[The men refuse to fire. Exit.]*

ACT IV.

―――――・――――

SCENE I.—Limerick, September, 1691—The walls and battlements — Hills in the distance—Thomond Bridge—Treaty Stone—Sentry on guard—Irish Flag. Trumpets sound.

―――――・――――

LORD MOUNTCASHEL, ...General of the Irish Army.
MARSHALL LUXEMBURGH, Commander-in-Chief of French Troops.
SARSFIELD, EARL OF LUCAN,. ...Major Gen'l of the Irish Army.
DILLON,...
O'NEIL,... ....
SIR DERMOD O'BRIEN,.....Colonel of the Fourth Irish Dragoons.
FATHER O'CARROLL,..... ..Chaplain to the Mountcashel Family.
MICHAEL O'RYAN,................ Sergeant in Sarsfield's Own.
ONEY SHEEHAN,................................An Irish Piper.
TIM O'CONNOR,....................Of the Kilkenny Rangers.
O'CARROLL OF NENAGH,.............Leader of the Rapparees.
GENERAL REVIGNY, ... A Huguenot.
GENERAL LEEVISON, ...Commander of the Dutch Blue Guards.
COLONEL HERBERT,.......... ....Of King William's Army.
SIR TOBY BUTLER,..........Commander of Ormond's Yeomanry.
STAFF OFFICERS, ...
OFFICERS, SOLDIERS, RAPPAREES, YOEMEN, &c. ....
LADY EVILEEN MACCARTHY,.......Daughter of Lord Mountcashel.
NORAH O'LEARY,..... ....Foster-sister of Lady Evileen.

――― ― ――

Enter Sarsfield, O'Brien, O'Neil and Officers.

Staff Officer.—General, a flag of truce from the enemy.

Sarsfield.—Ride out, sir, and conduct the bearer to our presence.

[*Enter Revigny and Leevison.*]

Sars.—Well, gentlemen, what greeting bring you from your master?

Rev.—My Lord, General Ginkle is anxious to avoid the useless shedding of blood. He sends you terms both honorable and generous; and when you learn the glad tidings that reached our camp this morning, your Lordship will see the folly of continuing this struggle further. O'Donnell has surrendered to Marlborough, and has taken his departure for Spain.

Sars.—Impossible! O'Donnell! No, I cannot believe it, Revigny; he will be the last Irish soldier to sheath his sword.

Rev.—I pledge you my honor as a soldier that it is true. [*Takes a dispatch from his breast and hands it to Sarsfield.*]

Sars. [*Reads.*]—O my country! now, indeed, thy trials accumulate; but we will still be faithful to thee. Gentlemen, bear to General Ginkle our refusal to accept his terms. Tell him that we will hold this proud old city for Ireland against all comers.

Rev.—My Lord I regret your resolution and bid you adieu.

Sars.—Good morning, gentlemen. [*Enter guards.*] Conduct these gentlemen to their lines. [*Turns to O'Brien.*]

> O'Brien! If we a treaty make,
> Will England her compact keep?
> If England dare these kingdoms to unite,
> Allegiance is no more her monarch's right.
> Sooner than from my country's cause depart
> I'd clasp her independence to my heart;
> This sword all ties with Briton would unbind,
> And fling the foul connection to the wind;
> And, when reclining on the bed of death,
> Ere this frail dust should yield its struggling breath,
> Like him who swore his son to endless hate,
> And thirst for vengeance on the invader's state,
> Each lisping boy indignantly I'd swear,
> By every pledge, by every oath that e'er
> Could bind his spirit, never to forego
> The bitterest hatred to his country's foe.
> Our country fallen—her liberty, her fame,
> Would lie entomb'd in England's hated name;
> On other shores would Erin's sons seek fame.

Her commerce vanished, her strength decayed,
No more within her noble deserted halls
To splend'rous feast the smile of welcome calls ;
Disease and death would soon o'erwhelm
A brave, a fertile and an ancient realm.

Ah no, O'Brien, we at least England's livery will
never wear. Its red glare would haunt our consciences
and sting us deep for our infamy.

[*Enter staff officer.*]

Staff Of.—My Lord I bring sad news,—the Duke
of Tyrconnell is dead.

Sars.—Dead! Then, indeed, James's cause is lost
for ever.

Staff Off.—Your presence is requested at the castle.
[*Exit all.*]

[*Enter funeral cortege, band playing the Adeste
Fidelis, then a detachment of the Royal Irish Foot
Guards—coffin borne on the muskets of six soldiers ;
Sarsfield, Sir Dermod. Dillon and officers as chief
mourners ; detachments from other regiments bring up
the rear. As the cortege is passing the long roll is
beaten, canonading and musketry is heard.*]

Sars.—Halt.

[*They lay down the coffin. Exit all but Serg't O'R.*

Serg't O'R.—Bad luck to yees, but yees might have
dacent manners, and let the poor corpse be buried in
quietness ; but its not in yees to do anything dacint,
so its not, never was nor never will be. Ah, God
presarve our people.

*A shell falls near the coffin ; Serg't O'R. lifts it
and throws it over the walls.*]

Serg't O'R.—Ah, you murderin' villin, go back to
the dirty blackguards that sent you. [*Funeral march
resumed.*]

[*Trumpets sound. Enter Sars., Sir Dermod, Dillon
and officers.*]

Staff Off.—My Lord, a large force of the enemy's
cavalry surprised Brigadier-Gen'l Clifford's command
at Annabeg, at day-break this morning, and have
made a lodgment on the Clare side of the Shannon.

Sars.—Order him under arrest, sir, at once. Such negligence must be severely punished. Now, indeed, our position is most critical. Coward or traitor he must be, to thus allow the enemy to cross the river and cut off our supplies, when he should have exercised the most sleepless vigilence. Yes, he is one of that party who would maintain the foul connection on any terms, no matter how degrading to our national honor. This imbecile has given to the enemy a weapon more terrible than all his legions. Starvation stares us in the face; but, gentlemen, a true soldier never despairs: Ginkle will find us awake and at our posts, ready to drive back his hordes. From the old Castle of St. John let the harp without the crown be thrown to the breeze! Under its beloved folds we can die as befits soldiers.

[*Enter staff officer.*]

Staff Off.—A flag of truce, my Lord.

Sars.—Conduct the gentlemen to our presence.

[*Enter General Revigny and Leevison.*]

Gen. Rev.—His majesty has graciously commanded us to offer for your acceptance, terms at once honorable, just and merciful. First, a full and complete amnesty; perfect religions equality guaranteed; the troops to march out with all the honors of war, the flag of England placed on one side, and the flag of France on the other; the soldiers to select freely under which standard they will serve.

[*Sarsfield consults with his officers*]

Sars.—Are these terms sent in good faith, sir?

Gen. Rev.—The Royal word is irrevocably pledged to the faithful carrying out of all the conditions of the Treaty as soon as signed by his Majesty's commissioners on one part, and your Lordship's on the other. And here your lordship, let me offer you, by the express command of General Ginkle, a commission in his Majesty's service, with a pension of six thousand crowns a year to the Generals. Leevison and myself add our personal entreaty to accept his generous offer.

Sars.—Many thanks, Revigny, for your generous

conduct, but I cannot accept his offer.   Under William's rule things will be so changed; the liberty of
our people will be curtailed, cramped and clogged by
a foreign parliament, the red will supplant the green,
the shamrock, small and fertile as it is, will be tram-
pled out of the land of our fathers.   No, Revigny, my
heart would sicken and die under such a regime.   In
good King Louis' dominions my comrades can, with
the green flag unfurled and borne proudly, march side
by side with the flag of Imperial France.   What say
you gentlmen ?   [*All the officers cheer.*]

Officers.—You speak our sentiments and resolve,
General.

[*Sarsfield advances to the Treaty Stone, on which he
signs the celebrated Treaty of Limerick, 3rd October,
1691.*]

Sars.—It is done in good faith on our part, let the
troops be marched out to select their future flag.

Rev.—His Majesty has consented to your embarkation on the French fleet.

Sars.—Thanks, General.

[*Enter Leerison and Sir Dermod.*]

Sars.—Well, have the troops made their selection ?

Sir D.—Yes, General, nineteen thousand seven hundred and fifty-five enlist under the banner of France,
five soldiers under the English.

Sars.—Nobly done, brave boys; but what a sacrifice
to thus leave the land of their birth, with all its kindred
and loving ties, fathers, mothers, wives and sisters; but
the enemies of our race on many a battle-field shall
yet feel our vengeance.

Sir D.—Everything is ready for our embarkation

Sars.—Then let the troops march.

[*By this time the stage is crowded with women, the
wives, mothers, and children of the soldiers—the loud
cry of och hone, och hone, resounds on every side.*]

Sars.—Now, good father, we crave thy blessing.

[*The soldiers and people all kneel—the priest blesses
them—they all rise.*]

Sars.—Now, sweet land, farewell. Farewell thou majestic Shannon. Farewell holy hills of sweet Mayo, where in childhood's days I often strayed to gaze on thy old and venerable abbeys. May God and his saints protect you, my own dear fatherland, good land, green land, dear Ireland—though we must leave you, may God's dew brighten all thy vales; His sun kiss every hill—and though henceforth our nights and days in strange lands must be passed, our hearts and our prayers will be ever at your command, farewell.

[*Sarsfield and his Generals advance to where the barge is in waiting—the women cling to the soldiers—Sarsfield and Officers step into the boat—The long roll is beaten—the soldiers break from their wives and mothers, and fall into line—the Officers give the command, March!—They march off the stage, amidst the cries of the women.*]

SCENE II.—*Camp of the Irish Brigades in the service of France—Eve of the Battle of Steinkirk—Enter Sarsfield and Sir Dermot.*

Sir D.—I bring you glad tidings, Lord Mountcashel has escaped from Carrickfergus. God grant he may reach the friendly shores of France in safety, as I see the English offer a reward of five thousand pounds for his apprehension.

Sars. [*takes Sir Dermot's hand*]—This is indeed good news, dear friend. I have been planning an expedition to Ireland.

Sir D.—To Ireland! General?

Sars.—Yes, listen. At Saint Maloes there is a French Skipper who has made several trips to Ireland, knows every inlet of the Shannon; in your Regiment you have several men from Ballymore, can you select one competent and faithful?

Sir D.—Let me see. Ah, yes, General. There is Sergeant O'Ryan, a good soldier, and Lady Evileen's foster sister's lover.

Sars.—That's the man, send him to me at once.

[*Exit Sir Dermod.*

Sars.—Yes, we must at least make the attempt to rescue this fair girl from the clutches of our treacherous enemy. .

[*Enter Sergeant O'Ryan.*]

Sars.—You are a Ballymore boy.

Serg't O'R.—Yes, General.

Sars.—Know the surroundings of the Castle?

Serg't O'R.—Ah, thin, General jewel, there's not a stone in the ould spot that Mickey Ryan l asn't made his acquaintance with; shure I could count every stone on my fingers for you.

Sars.—Well, then take this letter to Captain De Villesten of Saint Maloes, owner of a French lugger. give it to him—he will take you to the Shannon. When you arrive there, give him all the information in your power, you will then assume some disguise, gain an entrance into the castle, and communicate with father O'Carroll, and arrange with him for the escape of the Lady Evileen. Once on board the lugger, with a fair wind, you will soon reach the shores of La Belle France. Take this money, use it freely to gain the object we have so much at heart. Depart at once, loose not a moment.

[*Exit Serg't O'R.*]

[*Enter staff officer and hands dispatch to Sarsfield, who reads.*]

"23rd July, 1692.

"General, you will advance your whole force with all possible dispatch to Steinkirk, where you will have the pleasure of again meeting your old foe, William of Orange. Accept the assurance of our high esteem.

"LUXEMBURGH."

Sars. [*turns to his officers*]—Gentlemen, glorious news. We'll march to-night. With the rising of to-morrow's sun we'll again measure swords with our faithless enemy. Let the memory of our wrongs nerve every arm. Remember Limerick. Gentlemen, you will summon your officers and give your instructions. Let our battle-cry be "Garryowen, death, or glory."

SCENE III.—*Clanmacnoise, on the Shannon—Round towers and ancient ruins—Sentry on guard.*

Sentry [*Tim O'Connor*].—Ah, bad luck to their soldierin'. Shure I tould them a thousand times they'd never make a yoeman out of me. I'll light the pipe any how. It will be a consolation to me in this desolate spot—not a house or shebeen, man or beast, within five miles of me. By the great gun of Athlone, but if the grand rounds don't come soon I think I'll give them the slip. Shure, God forgive me for carry-ing a gun against the poor ould country, but shure it's against my will I do it, any how. Whist! What's that! [*puts up his pipe.*] Bedad it's the ould thief himself. I'll just drop behind this tree, so that he can't see me now I spake to him. [*Enter Sir Toby, attended by orderly*] Who's making that noise?

Sir T.—The rounds, you blackguard.

Tim O'C.—What rounds?

Sir T.—The grand rounds, you rascal.

Tim O'C.—Pass on grand rounds, and God save you kindly [*putting his pipe again in his mouth*].

Sir T.—Damn your soul you blackguard, where are you? Show yourself this moment or I'll have you shot like a dog.

Tim O'C.—Och then, Gineral jewel, why didn't you say that afore [*comes from behind the tree*]. Here

5*

I am, and a cowld place I have of it; only for the pipe I'd be lost intirely.

Sir T. [*laughing*]—You are a droll sentry.

Tim O'C.—Begorra, it's little fun is left in me with your drilling and parading, and blackguarding about the roads all night.

Sir T.—Is this a proper way to salute the grand rounds?

Tim O'C.—Divel a better ever they taught me.

Sir T.—See here, sir, the next time your officer passes this way, it will be your duty to present arms to him.

Tim O'C.—Arrah, it's jokin' you are.

Sir T.—No, sir, as you might find out to your cost, if I brought you to a court-martial.

Tim O'C.—Well, there's no knowing what they may be up to, but if that's all, shure I'll do it with all the veins of my heart, Gineral, whenever you come this way again,—long life to your honor.

Sir T.—Now you speak like a soldier. I will soon be this way again. Mind you don't forget proper respect to your general. [*Exit Sir Toby, but immediately returns.*] You haven't seen any of these wild geese from France?

Tim O'C.—Och, the divil a living thing, your honor, man, beast, or chicken.

Sir T.—Well, keep a sharp look out, for it is rumored that some French luggers have been seen in the Shannon. [*Exit Sir Toby.*

Tim O'C.—Och, bad luck to the ould thief. Aha! Maybe it is some poor boy from the Brigade stealin' in to see a desolate mother or wife that was left behind. Ah, thin, if he thinks Tim O'Connor is the boy to stop him he niver made a bigger mistake, the ould hypocrite [*takes off his hat*]. Oh, may God bless the boys of the Brigade, and Sarsfield, their gineral. [*A voice is heard to say* "Amen. It's a poor parish can't afford a clerk." *Enter Serg't O'Ryan disguised as a fisherman.*] Good Saint Bridget defend me! Who are you, or where did you come from?

Serg't O'R.—I am Sergeant O'Ryan, of Sarsfield's

Own, come from France to see the only colleen I ever
loved, and to save from a terrible fate one of Erin's
fairest and best beloved daughters, the Lady Evileen
of Mountcashel. In so holy and noble a mission I ask
your assistance, and if the Celtic blood that pours
through your veins has not been contaminated by the
livery you wear, you will not refuse me. No, you
will not—you cannot.

Tim O'C.—Fly! the soldiers will be here soon.
Though it is my duty to stop you, I cannot do it.
Go, I beseech you, avick.

Serg't O'R.—But the countersign. I cannot enter
the castle without it.

Tim O'C. [*hesitates*]—But I have taken an oath
not to divulge and to be loyal.

Serg't O'R.—Yes, but you took it against your will,
to save the bit of land that belonged to your fore-
fathers. Think you that is binding on your conscience? What care our persecutors for oaths? Have
they not broken faith with us over and over again?
Witness Limerick. The ink had not dried on the
treaty when our perjured enemies, with brazen ef-
frontery, outraged its most solemn obligations, con-
fiscated our lands, insulted and outraged our mothers,
sisters and wives, passed laws to cripple our industry
and commerce, branded our holy religion as barbarous
and idolatrous, and our venerable and beloved clergy
hunted like wolves and savage beasts! Oh! if there
is in your heart one drop of the blood of our brave
Celtic race, you will not refuse me the favor which I
ask.

Tim O'C.—[*deeply moved by Michael's appeal, puts
out his hand*]—Come close to me. It is—it is——
" Enniskillen!" Fly! Delay not a second as you
value your life. [*Exit Serg't O'R. Tim resumes his
post of sentry.*] By the piper I wonder if ould Sir
Toby will bother me any more this night with his
grand rounds. Bedad I'll light the pipe. Whist!—
what's that? If it's not the ould thief himself it's his
ghost. The Lord preserve us, but I'd sooner see him
alive than dead any how. Aha, here he comes; but I'll

be up to him this time [*takes up his gun and fixes his accoutrements*]. Oh, by all that's wonderful but he sees me, but I'll be afore him.

[*Enter Sir Toby. Tim presents his musket at him, keeping him well covered.*]

Sir T.—Sentry! sentry!

Tim O'C.—Bedad I hear, avick.

Sir T.—Do you want to murder me, you rascal? Don't you see its the Grand Rounds.

Tim O'C.—To be shure, I do.   [*still keeping him covered with his musket.*]

Sir T.—The ruffian will shoot me.

Tim O'C—Divil a fear, barrin it does'nt go off be itself, an' in truth if it does, its your own fault for putting guns in the hands of the likes of me; did'nt I tell you, you could'nt make a yeoman of Tim O'Conor, and if you are murdered, your murder be on your own head, avick, you can't deny that I often asked you for my discharge. Oh murdher, take care now Sir Toby, my hand is getting shaky from keeping her in so long, take care now I tell you.

Sir T.—The rascal will shoot me. Down with your gun, sir. No officer's life is worth a rush with a gun in the hands of such an omadhaun. Lay down your gun sir, and go to your home, let me never see your face in the Rangers again. Go, you are discharged, sir.

[*Tim gives a loud cheer, gives the gun a pitch. Exit.*]

Sir T.—Mighty glad to get rid of the rascal. I think I had a narrow escape from the omadhaun. What's that noise? [*Oney rushes on the stage—puts his arms round Sir Toby—puts a noose round his arms.*]

Oney.—Ah, I have you at last after long and weary sarchin' and watchin'. Oh mother jewel, you will soon be avenged, look down on your poor boy this day.

Sir T.—My good man, you surely would not injure me. Untie my arms, have mercy, have mercy.

Oney.—Aha! aha! how you mock the holy word; mercy, is it. What mercy had you, when you with your murderin' yeomin set fire to our little cabin, that sheltered us from the rains and storms of Winter.

Mercy, is it, and when struggling to escape from the scorchin' and suffocatin' flames and smoke, I snatched the almost lifeless body of my poor aged mother, lifted her in my arms jumped from the window, and again breathed the free air of heaven. Mercy, is it! Then with fiendish, hellish villany you cried, fire! I felt her heart's blood flow down my cheek, and swore an oath to be revenged. Long and weary has been my watch for you. Mercy, is it! you gave none, you'll get none, this minute you die. [*Oney presents a pistol at his head.*]

Sir T.—Oh, for the love of heaven do not murder me, you shall have riches, money, honors, everything, but do not murder me. Oh, murder! help! help!

Oney.—Aha! aha! you may cry but nothing but the winds hear you, die you must, blood for blood. [*Presents his pistol.*]

Sir T.—Help! help! mercy!

[*Enter Norah O'Leary.*]

Norah.—Mercy, who cries for mercy? [*Sir Toby rushes to her, clings around her feet, cries to her to save him.*]

Norah.—Oney, avick machree, would you commit murder? Oh, do not disgrace the good old cause.

Oney.—Stand away, Norah; what mercy had he for my poor ould mother, that never injured a human being. Stand away, I bid yea, for I'm mad, die he must. [*Norah catches his arm*]

Norah.—Oh, Oney, Oney, do not stain your hands with his blood, leave him to a higher judge.

Oney.—Stand aside, Norah, or your blood will be on my head too; stand aside, I bid ye.

Norah.—Oh, merciful heaven, he's mad. Good Saint Bridget, strengthen me—yes—I have it [*puts her hand in her bosom, takes a cross from her neck—puts it between Oney and his victim—it acts like magic.*

Norah.—That is the symbol of mercy and christianity, leave him to God, Oney, avick machree, and God will bless you. [*She puts the cross in his hands, draws him to the other side of the stage—voices are heard. Enter O'Carroll, attended by his rapparees.*]

O'Carroll.—This way, who have we here? A lady, eh? Who's this fine gentleman with the red coat? As I live, Sir Toby Butler, the very man we are most happy to see. Sir Toby, you are our prisoner, come, there's no use in making resistance, the poor people will be rid of the scourge for some time at least, come along, Oney, my boy, we may want your services. Can the O'Carroll do any favor for the fair Norah?

Norah.—Thank you sir, no; I must go to the castle, my Lady will be uneasy till I return.

O'Carroll.—How does the fair Lady Evileen?

Norah.—Heart broken and sad. She weeps for her lover. [*A drum is heard.*]

O'Carroll.—Ha! the red coats are astir. Farewell, you may soon again hear from O'Carroll, the Rapparee.   -   [*Exit.*]

SCENE IV.—*Lady Evileen's Boudoir in Ballymore Castle — Father O'Carroll, Lady Evileen, and Norah.—Lady Evileen weeping.*

Father O'C.—Patience, my child, I have a communication to make that will tax all your fortitude, accustomed as we have been to scenes of woe and bloodshed, but this last affliction will, I fear, be too much for your already over-burthened heart.

Lady E.—Say on, good father, I am prepared for the worst.

Father O'C.—Well, your respected father has been detected in the act of corresponding with the French government, giving plans and information, been tried, and by a court-martial found guilty, and sentenced to be hung like a common felon.

Lady E.—Oh, honorable father, why did you leave yourself in our enemy's power? [*turns to Norah, embraces her and weeps.*]

Norah.—My poor darling—God grant you consolation my poor child.

[*Lady Evileen recovers*] I will go to England, throw myself at William's feet—he will have mercy; Oh, father dear, to be hung like a thief! from such a disgrace to our house, good Saint Bridget deliver us. I will depart at once. My cloak and hat, Norah.

Father O'C.—Patience, my child; long before you could reach England your father would be cold in his grave. Listen, when the dispatch arrived, I sought Colonel Herbert, pointed out to him the agony you would suffer, begged of him to depart for Dublin and at least stay the execution for a day.

Lady E.—And he refused.

Father O'C.—Not so, my child, he has already departed for Dublin.

Lady E.—Thank heaven, there is yet some hope.

Father O'C.—Yes, but the fulfilment of that hope is in your own hands, and depends on your own decision.

Lady E.—Good father, I do not understand you: what sacrifice would I not make to save a loving and kind parent from such an ignominious death. Name it.

Father O'C.—Now, my child, listen. You know Colonel Herbert loves you—has loved you since first he entered this castle as a prisoner of war. He offered his hand and fortune. You refused, of course, being betrothed, to the late lamented Sir Dermod. [*Lady Evileen weeps on Norah's shoulder.*] You know his brother's influence at the Court of William. It is now for you to say that you will become his bride and your father is saved, and restored to his child and to liberty.

Lady E.—Mercy! mercy! His bride! Ah! I was to have been a bride!—the bride of one of my own race and kindred. But he's gone! gone!—died fighting for his country! He's gone! Oh! Dermod, my love! my heart is yours! Love another I never will. I cannot!—I cannot! Any other sacrifice—death, good father; death is preferable.

Father O'C.—Then the last of the princely Mountcashels dies a felon's death.   His child could save him, but will not.

Lady E.—Oh, mercy! mercy! I—I—consent.

       [*Lady Eveline swoons into Norah's arms.*]

Father O'C.—Poor child, I pity her. But I must away; there's not a moment to be lost.

               [*Exit Father O'Carroll.*]

Norah.—My lady, do listen to your Norah. Be comforted, alannah. Joy of my heart, do speak one word to your own Norah, that would die for you.

Lady E. [*recovering*]—Forgive me, Norah. I feel much better now—much better, Norah.

Norah.—Ah, that's a jewel. It does my heart good to hear you speak so. Shure the poor master will be saved. The thought of that alone must be a consolation to your poor broken heart.

   [*Enter Col. Herbert, officers, and Father O'Carroll.*]

Father O'C.—The time has arrived to fulfil your promise, my child.

   [*Lady Evileen weeps. The ceremony proceeds till the priest says:* "And if any one has aught to say that they should not be joined in wedlock, let him speak." *Just at this moment drums beat, a volley of musketry is heard, and sounds of conflict. Enter Serg't O'Ryan through the window.*]

Serg't O'R.—I forbid the bans, in the name of Sir Dermod O'Brien, this lady's affianced husband.

   [*Michael rushes to the side of Lady Evileen and Norah. Michael and Norah embrace.*]

Col. H. [*draws his sword*]—Fool and babbler! How come you here? Sir Dermod O'Brien is dead. Let the ceremony proceed.

Serg't O'R.—Liar! he is living, and has the honor to hold a Brigadier-General's commission in the service of his most gracious majesty, Louis the 14th, King of France and the Netherlands.

         [*Lady Evileen and Norah embrace.*]

Lady E.—Norah, dear Norah, this is indeed joyful intelligence.   [*Norah folds her to her bosom.*]

Col. H.—Scoundrel, I'm not to be cheated [*turns to his officers.*] Let all the outlets from the castle be strictly guarded, and see that no one escapes. Lady Evileen, I'll bind you to our contract. If you refuse, your father shall swing like a dog from the gallows.

Serg't O'R.—False again! Her father has escaped, and is, thank God, safe in France.

Col. H.—Then she shall never leave this castle. Guards! secure this babbler!

Michael [*draws his sword*].—Stand back, now, ye murderin' pack of spalpeens. By Saint Patrick, the first man that lays a finger on the fair lady—[*a volley of musketry. Sounds of conflict again heard.*]

Col. H.—More treason [*some one enters the window.*] Fire!

[*Enter Oney from the window, wounded and bleeding—staggers into the arms of Father O'Carroll.*]

Oney.—I'm dying, father [*puts his hand in his breast—gives a despatch Sergeant O'Ryan comes to Oney's assistance while Father O'Carroll reads*]:

" Dublin Castle.

" *To Colonel Herbert, and to all whom it may concern, greeting :*

"On receipt of this our Order of Council, you will give instant and safe conduct to the Lady Evileen McCarthy, chaplain, and suite, to our city of Limerick, then and there to embark for France. You are further enjoined to the faithful carrying out of these our Orders in Council, as the valuable life of our well beloved brother, Sir Toby Butler, is held hostage for its faithful execution.

"Given under our hand and seal, this 12th day of March, 1692.   " ORMOND."

Father O'C.—Sunshine at last. God's justice is sometimes slow, but sure. Sir, I present you with the order from the Viceroy for our immediate release. We'll take our departure for France at once.

Col. H.—'Tis a forgery, sir. Some cunning trick or devise to cheat me.

Father O'C.—Examine the signature, sir. You
will find it genuine and correct.

[*Colonel Herbert disputes.*]

Oney [*supported by Sergeant O'Ryan, and fast
sinking*].—Oh, mother jewel, your poor boy is coming!
Let me gaze on the colors once more before I die!
God bless the green! [*kisses it*] I die happy! Mother,
I'm coming!   [*Oney dies.*]

Father O'C.—Poor, faithful creature. Oh, my
country, who will despair of the future, when the
humblest of thy children thus sacrifice their lives in
thy service. [*Oney is borne off the stage.*] Well, sir,
are you satisfied? If not, read this [*hands a paper to
Col. Herbert.*]

Col. II. [*reads*]—"If in one hour after sunset, the
Lady Evileen, chaplain, and suite are detained in the
castle, Sir Toby Butler dies.

(Signed)   "O'CARROLL, of Nenagh."

Officer.—Both signatures are genuine—let them depart.

[*Colonel Herbert covers his face with his hands,
while Father O'Carroll leads the way, followed by
Lady Evileen and Norah, Serg't O'Ryan bringing up
the rear.*

SCENE V.—*Camp of the Irish Brigade in the service of France, the eve of the battle of Landen, July
28, 1693—Irish and French flags displayed—
Sentry on guard—Sarsfield seen sitting in his tent—
Maps displayed.*

Sars.—It is most possible the enemy will push on to
Langden; Luxemburgh, in that event, must commence
the attack.

[*Serg't O'Ryan's voice is heard singing*] :

"Oh, the English ran away,
  Says the Shan Van Vocht,
And the French they gained the day,
  Says the Shan Van Vocht"

Sent.—Sergeant O'Ryan wishes an audience.

Sars.—Admit him sir. [*Enter Sergeant O'Ryan.*] Well, Sergeant, what news? I hope your mission has been successful.

Serg't O'R.—Ah, long life to you, General! glorious news.

Sars.—The Lady Evileen?

Serg't O'R.—Is safe and sound, yer honor.

Sars.—In France?

Serg't O'R.—In the village; and thinks every minute a century 'till she sees her father.

Sars.—She shall not have long to wait. Sergeant, you are a noble fellow, and well deserve the thanks of a fond father.

Serg't O'R.—Ah, General jewel, where's the Ballymore boy that wouldn't lay down his life for the fair daughter of Mountcashel!

Sars.—And your own colleen, Sergeant?

Serg't O'R.—Is safe, yer honor, with the Lady Evileen. Many thanks, yer honor, for asking for the colleen. Father O'Carroll is with the creatures.

Sars.—Then let them come over to the camp; I will arrange a surprise.

Serg't O'R.—Long life to you, General.

[*Exit Serg't O'R.*]

Sars.—My dear old friend little dreams of the happiness that's in store for him. And Sir Dermod O'Brien. Ah! it will be a joyful meeting indeed. [*Writes a dispatch and hands it to the sentry.*] Yes, it will be a delightful surprise.

[*Enter Lord Mountcashel & Sir Dermod O'Brien. Sarsfield advances to meet them and takes them by the hand.*]

Sars.—I have sent for you, my friends, as I wish to have the pleasure of your company. Having invited some old friends to supper, I wished you to join our little social circle.

Mountcashel.—Many thanks, General; nothing will give greater pleasure.

Sars.—Then I will introduce you.

[*Enter Father O'Carroll, Lady Evileen, Norah and Sergeant O'Ryan. Sarsfield advances and takes Lady Evileen's hand.*]

Sars.—My Lord, your child.

[*Lady Evileen rushes into the arms of her father. Sarsfield and Sir Dermod O'Brien shake hands with Father O'Carroll. Lord Mountcashel advances with Lady Evileen, who rushes into Sir Dermod's arms. Norah and Serg't O'Ryan embrace.*]

Lord M.—Norah, my faithful girl, happy and delighted to see you; and you, Sergeant, a thousand thanks for your courage and devotion. Norah! here, give me your hand. [*Places it in Sergeant O'Ryan's.*] Here, my brave fellow, take her, love her, cherish her.

Serg't O'R.—God bless you, my Lord, shure I'll do all a poor boy can do to make her as happy as the day is long. [*Embraces Norah.*]

Norah.—Michael, darling, my heart will burst with happiness.

Serg't O'R.—Oh don't let it my darling; keep it safe 'til your poor boy takes full possession of it, alannah.

The long roll is beaten; trumpets sound, and distant cannonading heard.]

Sars.—Ha! the enemy is moving: well, they will find Luxemburgh prepared for them. Father, you will retire to the village with the ladies.

[*Lady Evileen takes leave of her father and Sir Dermod.*]

Lady E.—May heaven this day shield all we love from harm or danger.

[*Exit Lady Evileen, Norah and Father O'Carroll.*]
[*Enter Marshal Luxemburgh.*]

Marshal L.—Well, gentlemen, His Majesty of England thinks he has stolen a march on us, but for once he's mistaken. Luxemburgh never sleeps when the enemies of France are near. [*Enter staff officer.*

Staff Off.—The enemy has advanced large masses of infantry on our left centre; our troops have been overpowered and were obliged to give ground.

Marshal L.—To give ground, sir! Ride back; they must not give ground, sir! they must hold their position.

[*Enter staff officer.*]

Staff Off.—General, nothing can stay the victorious columns of the enemy. The Household Troops have given way.

Marshal L.—The honor and glory of France is dimmed. Forward, my brave Sarsfield, to the rescue!

[*Sarsfield and his officers draw their swords.*]

Sars.—Now, my countrymen, our time has come. France calls us to the rescue of its old and glorious flag—the flag that gave us shelter, welcome, and hospitality. Let every man grasp his sword with a determination to wield it while one gasp of life gives strength. Yes, we'll plant ourselves like a wall of granite before the enemy, and say to those haughty English: "Thus far hast thou come, but shalt come no further." Let the memories of our wrongs and sufferings nerve every arm. Remember Limerick! Forward!

[*Exit Sarsfield, Sir Dermod, Luxemburgh, and officers.—The sounds of the conflict are heard on the stage.—Enter Lord Mountcashel, wounded.—Cheers are now heard.*]

Lord M.—Those cheers are a good omen.
[*Enter some French officers.*]
Lord M.—Well, gentlemen, what news?
Officers.—The victorious columns of the enemy are checked. [*Tremendous cheers are heard—then strikes out the soul-stirring air of Garryowen.—Enter Luxemburgh and Staff.—Enter Sir Dermod and officers.—Soldiers bearing Sarsfield, wounded.*]

Luc—Our victory is complete [*advances to Sars-field, takes his hand.*] My Lord, the French Nation, its King, and the French Army, thank you and your brave countrymen. France will ever gratefully remember their gallant behaviour on the bloody field of Landen.

Sars.—We did but our duty. [*He swoons—all gather around. Enter Sergeant O'Ryan, bearing some captured flags—lays them at Sarsfield's feet—Sarsfield is dying.—Sir Dermod, Lord Mountcashel, and all the Irish officers gather around him.*]

Sars.—My time is come, farewell, my comrades [*kisses the green flag*]. Ah, would to God, gentlemen, this was for Ireland ! [*dies*].

THE END.